The Grey Woman

*by
M J Hardy*

Copyrighted Material

Copyright © M J Hardy 2020

M J Hardy has asserted her rights under the Copyright, Designs and Patents Act 1988 to be identified as the Author of this work.

This book is a work of fiction and except in the case of historical fact, any resemblance to actual persons, living or dead, is purely coincidental.

All rights reserved. No part of this book may be reproduced or transmitted in any form without written permission of the author, except by a reviewer who may quote brief passages for review purposes only.

Contents

Have you Read
Prologue
Chapter One
Chapter Two
Chapter Three
Chapter Four
Chapter Five
Chapter Six
Chapter Seven
Chapter Eight
Chapter Nine
Chapter Ten
Chapter Eleven
Chapter Twelve
Chapter Thirteen
Chapter Fourteen
Chapter Fifteen
Chapter Sixteen
Chapter Seventeen
Chapter Eighteen
Chapter Nineteen
Chapter Twenty
Chapter Twenty-One
Chapter Twenty-Two
Chapter Twenty-Three
Chapter Twenty-Four
Chapter Twenty-Five
Chapter Twenty-Six

Chapter Twenty-Seven
Chapter Twenty-Eight
Chapter Twenty-Nine
Chapter Thirty
Chapter Thirty-One
Chapter Thirty-Two
Chapter Thirty-Three
Chapter Thirty-Four
Chapter Thirty-Five
Chapter Thirty-Six
Chapter Thirty-Seven
Epilogue
Note from the Author
Other books
Thankyou

HAVE YOU READ:

sjcrabb.com

The Girl on Gander Green Lane

The Husband Thief

Living the Dream

The Woman who Destroyed Christmas

Quote

Stop living in the shadows of others.
Break away and make your dreams become reality.
Tricia Inniss

I am the grey woman.
I walk in the shadows of other people's lives and have no life of my own to shout about. Nobody sees me because I shrink away into my own little world. I am a nothing, a nobody, and people like us don't draw attention to ourselves. We have nothing to shout about anyway, so we listen. Watch and listen and move in the shadows where the invisible people live.
But now my dreams have changed and I want more than I ever thought I deserved. I want what they have and I don't care how I get it. Money is a powerful aphrodisiac and the ruin of men. It sucks you in and promises the world and people will do anything to grasp it for themselves.
I am no exception.
It's time to venture out of the shadows and take what I want, and the secrets I have heard will get it for me.
Will I want what's waiting for me, or will I wish I had never left the shadows at all?

Prologue

Something's wrong. I feel it as soon I open my eyes. I can't see anything; there's only darkness. I feel cold and I'm shivering as a draft caresses my body with a chilling breeze. My limbs ache and I'm lying on something cold and hard and the smell - it's overpowering and I can't breathe.

Am I dreaming? I must be because this isn't where I fell asleep, where am I?

Something touches my leg and I open my mouth to scream, but no sound comes out. I'm screaming and screaming, but I must be deaf. I can't hear anything; all I can do is *feel*. My senses are shutting down one by one, and yet I hear the soft breathing of somebody nearby - *someone's here*.

A prickle of fear quickly gains momentum until I feel so afraid, I almost pass out. I feel sick and retch, but nothing happens. I try to move but can't. Am I paralysed or worse – dead?

Where am I? The stench is overpowering me, it smells familiar but I can't place it.

Then the pressure on my leg increases and I hear a soft, "She's coming round."

I try to put a face to the voice, but it all seems so distant. Then I hear a man's voice, louder, more urgent. "We don't have long."

What's happening, where am I?

Then I feel a liquid running down my leg that burns and I scream and this time my voice works, although it's weaker than normal. A sharp voice hisses, "Shut up, we are just cleaning you up to prepare you for transit."

Transit, what the hell is happening, who are these people?

I want to be sick; the smell is too intense and I retch. Then I feel a calm hand on my forehead and the man says, "She's burning up, how much did you give her?"

"The usual dose; she'll be fine."

I feel her hands all over me now. Scrubbing, kneading, burning and torturing. They move to my stomach and I wince as the pain grips me and she says angrily, "She's damaged; they may reject her."

"No, they won't care. She'll look a lot worse by the time they've finished with her."

I can't move and I can't talk. What the hell is happening?

I start to shiver, I am so cold, so sick and in so much pain it consumes my entire body. It's too intense and I can't breathe. What is that smell?

Then I hear, "It's done, you can bring the truck around."

I hear movement, loud noises and the scraping of a heavy object across a concrete floor. The cold is intense and the pain hurts from the inside out.

Then I hear a whisper, a soft sound in my ear as she says, "It's time to go."

Go where, what is she talking about?

Somebody is lifting me, but still I can't move. Then another grabs my head and pulls it back by my hair. I cry out in pain and then the light hits me, blinding me as something is torn from my eyes. *I can see again.*

As my eyes focus and their faces swim into view, I stare at them in shock. "You!"

1
Three months earlier

The house feels cold. The clock radio beside my bed tells me it's time to get up, but my body begs to differ. Why leave the warm comfort of my bed for a routine that's becoming increasingly difficult every day?

The darkness surrounds me, and not just because the sun has decided to have a lie in. I'm not sure when the darkness decided to attach itself to me like an unwanted virus, but I can't remember when I last felt – normal.

Sighing, I swing my legs from the bed and shiver as the icy air bites. Steeling myself, I run for the shower, desperate to feel the warm jets of water shocking my body back to life and giving me some much-needed energy for the day ahead – I'll need it.

By the time I'm washed, dressed and ready, it's been exactly twenty minutes and I venture downstairs to carry out the final ritual before I leave for work. Breakfast.

As if on autopilot, I carry out the same routine that I do every morning of the week bar one. Sunday.

I flick the kettle on and while that boils make my cereal. It takes all of five minutes to make my breakfast and just as long to eat it. While I do, I flick on the television to watch the morning news.

The grave face that greets me tells me it's another day for bad news. Then again, there never appears to be a time when there isn't.

As I settle down with my cereal, I focus on what the woman who appears to have it all is saying.

"Melissa Roberts has been missing for three days and Police fear for her safety. Her family have held a press conference to plead for any information."

The picture switches to an elderly couple who look like a deer caught in the headlights as they stare at the camera with ashen faces and trembling lips. The man keeps on wringing his hands as he pleads for information on the whereabouts of his daughter. My heart goes out to them as I see the worry in their eyes mixed with nerves at being forced to address the nation on a subject they never thought would happen to them.

The door slams and I jump up, reaching for the kettle as if on autopilot. Then I fix a welcoming smile on my face as my husband heads wearily into the room. "Morning."

He just nods and slams the keys on the counter, and I can tell it's been another long night.

"It's bloody freezing out there. You'll need to wrap up."

I watch as he sinks down into the chair I have only just left and stares at the screen moodily. I'm not sure he even registers what they say as he stares blankly in front of him, seemingly wrapped in his own thoughts as always.

Handing him a steaming mug of tea, I say brightly, "How was it?"

"Quiet."

My heart sinks. "Oh."

He doesn't even look up as he takes the hot mug of tea and I say wearily, "I should get going then."

I'm not sure why I even bother because he never answers me. In fact, we don't have many conversations these days and I've always put it down to the fact we are like ships that pass in the night. He works while I sleep and vice versa. The only day we have off together is Sunday, and most of that is spent cleaning and doing the multitude of jobs that pile up throughout the week. We never socialise with other couples, and our life has become dull in the extreme. I tell myself that this is normal. The life they portray in magazines and on the television is the dream, not the reality. We are what passes as normal these days, and anyone that says differently is obviously lying. However, the only person I am fooling is myself because they are all around me. The people who blow my theory out of the water because I hear them talking. I hear their stories of a life well lived and see the excitement in their eyes as they spill another juicy tale to entertain their friends. These people have a life I can only dream of because mine appears to have set up residence in the deepest rut possible.

I call out, 'goodbye', as I head out the door but as usual get nothing in return.

Yes, my life has taken a path where nothing much ever happens and increasingly, I decide that I'm not ok with it.

"Morning Emma."

As I push open the door to Barrington's, the coffee shop I work in for most of the day, I feel the warm air hit me, welcoming me in from the cold. I look up and see Leah smiling sweetly at me as she works. "You look frozen, grab a coffee to warm you through."

"It's fine. It won't take long to warm up, I'll just get started."

Shrugging, she carries on preparing the cups for the morning rush and I stow my belongings and join her.

We work like this, side by side for most of the day, until we are replaced by the evening shift. Just Leah and me mainly, but then Hailey arrives for the afternoon rush and sometimes, if it's busy, the owner Calvin lends a hand.

Leah says in a low voice, "I see another girl's gone missing. That must be the third one this year already and it's only February."

"Do you think she's run away? I hope so, for her sake."

"Nah, too much of a coincidence. The police wouldn't hold a press conference if they thought she'd just run off. You could tell by her parents they weren't the sort of family with issues."

"How do you know that just by looking at them?"

I laugh and shake my head. "They may have a whole cupboard of issues that will soon come spilling out."

"No, they're normal people and normal people's issues usually involve paying the bills and missing the odd credit card payment. They don't file missing person reports and go on national television to plead for the safe return of a loved one, unless it's completely out of the normal running of their lives. It's sinister, you mark my words."

As I set out the cakes and pastries under the counter, I have to agree with her. I'm pretty sure those people would have covered every avenue possible before subjecting themselves to the spotlight that going on national television shines on you and my heart goes out to them. Hopefully, their daughter will show up and the nation will breathe a collective sigh of relief, but I doubt it. That never seems to happen, and I expect the next press conference will be to advise us of the body they've found in a secluded woodland or somewhere similar.

The door opens and my first customer of the day heads inside, shivering from the cold and I smile. "Morning sir, your usual?"

He nods and I set about making him the usual Americana he orders every single day. While he waits, he looks around him with the usual boredom and never appears to want to make conversation, even though we have met at the same time every day for the last two years. It's almost as if I'm invisible, and I doubt he would even recognise me if I passed him in the street.

As I hand him the hot beverage, he scans his card on the machine to pay without even looking at me. Then he takes his drink and joins the rest of the workers streaming into the city, all heading for the tower blocks of high finance.

I don't have time to be annoyed at his rudeness because he is no different to anyone else. They don't see me and yet I see them. Every last one of them because I am hungry for information. I listen to their idle chatter and pounce on every word. I look eagerly at their fine clothes and take in their appearance as they stand patiently waiting for a cup of something hot to accompany them to work. I relish their conversation mainly into their phones and wonder about the silent ones as they stand waiting, hunched inside their jackets avoiding eye contact with the rest of civilisation. Yes, I love my job because it indulges my hobby. People watching and the people that come in here are the ones who have it all – at least it appears that way.

I work in the city near Canary Wharf. The power house of London where the country really runs from. There is more money here than in the bank of England, and it oozes from every crack of every building surrounding Barrington's coffee shop. The women are dressed immaculately with the finest tailoring. The men are no exception and their clipped tones of an educated person make them far superior to me. I find myself emulating their accents where I can, trying to prove I'm one of them, but I'm not.

No, I'm Emma Carter from Croydon. Born into a life of near poverty with none of the help they have received along the way. I slotted into my position in life as is required and barely scraped an exam pass at school before meeting Ronnie Carter and marrying on my nineteenth birthday. We grabbed the council house we were given with greedy open arms and have scrimped and scraped to drag ourselves through life, telling ourselves that we are happy with our lives. I am not.

Ronnie drives a mini cab at night with the occasional day thrown in, and his only pleasure is the game of cards he attends at a friend's house once a week. While he works at night, I sleep and while he sleeps, I work in Barrington's and then move on to clean the very offices my customers migrate to everyday. By the time I return home, Ronnie has left and we don't think anything of it. In fact, if I was brutally honest, I prefer it that way. My own company has always been welcomed and any friends I had have either moved away, or found new ones because I work every hour I can and when I'm off, spend it cleaning my own home and preparing for the week ahead. No, I don't need friends because I surround myself with much more interesting lives every day and I lap up any small pieces of information they spill like a hungry animal.

As the line gets longer, my attention falls to the job and I set about feeding the workers with the fuel they need to make it into the office.

2

The morning passes quickly and soon the lunchtime rush hits. This is my favourite time of all because the workers take a minute to sit and chat and I move around the coffee shop clearing the tables and listening in on their conversations. I relish their tales of life in the steel-clad offices that cast their shadows over our lives. The very offices I enter as they leave and find myself trying to match the face with the job, which has become a favourite game.

At 1.05 pm on the dot, she appears and I feel the excitement grip me.

Claire Quinn is the personal assistant of Julian Landon. The big boss of Crossline Asset Management, one of the most successful companies in Canary Wharf. They trade in stocks and shares and I often see the euphoria on the faces of the traders as they make another killing, or the abject misery on the ones that fail and lose more money in one minute than I will make in a lifetime.

Crossline Asset Management is a world I can only dream about, and I dream a lot. If I could have one wish in life, it was that I was part of it. It's exciting, intoxicating and a world away from my own one and certainly not attainable to a woman like me.

I live out my fantasies by listening in for any information at all about a place I know nothing about and move across to clear the table near to the one Claire has taken up temporary residence at and listen as she speaks into her phone.

"Hey, it's done."

She listens and then laughs softly. "He was surprised, which made me laugh. For a man as clever as he is, he obviously didn't see this one coming."

I wipe the table and hang onto her every word. "One month. Hmm, he tried for longer but I told him we have plans and they don't include an extended notice period."

I hold my breath as she laughs softly. "Me too, babe. Have you heard from, William?"

Her conversation switches to another subject and I carry the tray laden with dirty mugs and plates back to the dishwasher. Notice - one month – she's leaving.

I feel a tingle of excitement as I sense change coming. Claire Quinn, personal assistant for the past five years to Julian Landon, is leaving. He won't like that, I'm sure of it. During the last five years I've built up quite the information database on the impressive Mr Landon, and I know he's a man who likes control. If his pa is leaving, it will force change and I'm guessing he will be angry at that. Even I can tell that Claire is good at her job. She is efficient, calm, controlled and polite. She carries out her role with good grace and a professionalism I aspire to everyday. I hear her conversations with her fellow workers and see the looks she receives in return. They are every bit as impressed with her as I am; I see it in their eyes and now she's leaving.

The news stirs something deep inside me. It's a feeling that's been growing for the last year or so that started with a small seed that has taken root and is now growing out of control. The seed of change that involves my own life. I'm not sure when the idea first hit me, but over the past few months it has increasingly occupied my mind.

I want more.

More than the life I have, more than the jobs I work hard at, more from my marriage and more than just routine in my life. I want what these people have, and I want the excitement that goes with it. Can I force change, am I really that brave? Dare I raise my head over the parapet and face the enemy head on?

Claire Quinn is leaving and I know this is my chance. I have prepared for this day and so, with an excitement that threatens to take me under, I make a decision. It's time.

As soon as I step foot over the threshold of my next port of call for the day, I feel different. This time I envisage myself entering these premises and making a different type of journey. Instead of heading to the basement, I see myself taking the elevator to the highest floor. Walking the carpeted hallways of the executive offices and taking my seat as the personal assistant to the most powerful man in the building. Yes, I dare to dream because I have thought of little else since lunchtime. It's a dream I never dared imagine, and now the idea is planted, it's taking off like a rocket.

"Evening, Emma."

As I head toward my locker, I see Lisa, my co-worker already shrugging into her overalls.

"I'm just not in the mood tonight, it's too cold and I think I'm coming down with that virus everyone's talking about."

Shaking my head, I bite back a smile. As hypochondriacs go, Lisa is one of the best.

"I'm sorry to hear that, maybe you should have called in sick."

"I wish I had that luxury. My rent's due, there's nothing in the fridge and I've seen a cute little skirt I want to buy online."

Grinning, I raise my eyes. "Oh, and Declan's back from holiday."

She pretends to look surprised.

"Is he, I didn't know?"

She has the grace to blush and I roll my eyes and turn away, stifling a grin. Lisa and Declan, the security guard in charge of the night shift, have the hots for each other and indulge their desires most nights. Lisa works the executive offices and I clean the ones on the floor below. I've seen Declan head up to find her on the premise of checking the offices. He takes exactly five minutes to check my floor and thirty to complete his sweep of the executive offices. Yes, Declan and Lisa have it all their own way and I couldn't care less. To my knowledge, they are both free agents and can do what they like. I suppose it's only a matter of time before they make it official, but it just reinforces the fact that everyone else is having a good time where I am not.

Although, I'm glad it's her rather than me because I've always found Declan a little creepy. He has those eyes that strip you bare and proposition you with no words spoken. I've heard stories of him at Barrington's from the junior secretaries, all convinced he's the man of their dreams. I suppose he's good looking in a bad boy sort of way. Rugged and dominant, the usual alpha male that the girls appear to love these days. I'm guessing he spends more time in the gym than at work because he always looks pumped and ready to crush an opponent into dust should the need arise. Yes, Declan Cole is the sort of man that drives women's fantasies and Lisa is no exception it would seem.

Sighing to myself, I grab my cleaning trolley and head to the elevators. By now the offices should be clear, and if anyone's working late, I concentrate on the empty desks first. I watch Lisa head off with her trolley to the second bank of elevators, which lead to the executive offices. They even have their own method of transport there, which levitates them above the rest of the lowly workforce. I wonder what it's like up there, maybe one day I'll get to work that floor? If I have my way, I will be doing a very different job to the one I have now. Fingers crossed, anyway.

3

Tonight, as I work, I have a different job on my mind. Somehow, I need to apply for the position of Julian Landon's pa and it won't be easy.

As I clean the offices belonging to the staff of the man himself, I try to build a picture of the company I seek to join.

Waste bins are usually good information dumps, and I make sure to sift through every one of them for something that may help me.

I've amassed quite the database over the past year and passwords, telephone numbers and juicy titbits of gossip, have found their way into my notebook one way or another. I'm always careful not to be discovered as I enter the security code to a filing cabinet, or a password to the computer system. I'm not sure why I started doing it; maybe subconsciously it was for this very reason – to ease my application in securing the job I desire more than anything right now.

The sky is dark outside and the strip lighting of the office reveals my sad reflection as I work in the empty space. Silence is all around me, unless you count the sirens and general traffic outside of the city that never sleeps.

I match up the photos on the desks with the customers in Barrington's. For instance, Joey Matthews is seeing Katie Evans from accounting and I know she is married. I see the crumpled notes in the bins as they resort to the old-fashioned way of communicating, never dreaming for one moment that their rubbish would be so incriminating.

I know that Fenella Sullivan is planning on resigning because her boss is intimidating her and bullies her every hour of the day. I see the drafted letter detailing every conversation and reprimand given. They are then screwed into a ball and re-written as even more ammunition is added to the charge sheet.

Her boss, Miles Sinclair, is an oily piece of filth whose main ambition is to make it upstairs to the executive offices. He is currently pursuing Alice Vander Woods, who is the HR manager's assistant. His own wife and baby beam proudly from the silver frame on his desk, but I hear the conversation the two of them share when they think no one is listening as they hide from view in the corner booth in Barrington's.

Yes, I know everything about these people and could write a book on what goes on here. The trouble is, nobody would believe a word of it because it's so explosive, even I would doubt its authenticity.

However, now I need to put my knowledge to the test and use it to get me what I want because I will only get one shot and I can't afford to miss.

By the time I make it home, I'm exhausted. Ronnie left a couple of hours ago and I sigh as I re-heat the ready meal we appear to live on these days.

I know Ronnie grabs something out most nights and I'm usually so tired, food is the last thing on my mind.

However, tonight I have an extra shot of adrenalin and as soon as I've eaten, open my notebook to plot my next move. I need to plan this operation with a military precision because I don't have long. I want Claire Quinn's job more than life itself, and if I fail, it won't be through lack of trying.

Once I have my plan in place, I decide to grab half an hour of television before indulging in a long hot soak in the bath tub.

I make a mug of tea and settle down to watch the evening news and see the poor parents of the girl who went missing. My heart goes out to them as they plead once again for their daughter's safe return. The police officer that accompanies them looks serious and I can tell by the look in his eye he doesn't hold out much hope. I try to remember a positive outcome of one of these conferences and come up empty and my heart sinks as I picture their future and it's not a pleasant one.

However, sleep soon beckons and I head off to bed. Maybe tomorrow will bring better news, I hope so, for their sakes.

The next day it's obvious that word has got out because there's a buzz of excitement in Barrington's. The secretaries, personal assistants and receptionists are unusually talkative and as I listen in, every conversation regards the newly vacant position. I hear the receptionist Fiona Matthews discussing it with Sarah Stammers the temp from 'Hire it.' "You should apply, Sarah. You've got shed loads of experience and quite frankly, who wouldn't want to work for Julian Landon, the man's a god among men."

Sarah nods dreamily. "You can say that again. When are the applications closing?"

"Friday. It's on the internal vacancies board. I think they're opening it up to staff first and then a few agencies they use. Maybe yours is one of them."

Sarah looks thoughtful. "I'll call and see if they've heard anything. If they have, I'll get them to push my CV their way. Oh, I'd love to work here permanently. There is so much opportunity in Crossline and to be honest, I'm bored with just being in a place a few weeks at a time. Maybe this was meant to be, you know, right place, right time."

They drift away and I feel anxious. Sarah is good, she's also already proved her worth and would probably stand a good chance. Like Claire, she is presentable, efficient and easy on the eye. I'm guessing Mr Landon would be pleased as punch to have her working under him.

I think I'm on tenterhooks all day and listen eagerly for any snippet of information that I can use to my gain.

Claire herself appears as usual at 1.05, and orders her usual Americano with half fat milk, and I look at her with interest, trying to imagine myself in her place.

A woman behind her in the queue taps her on the shoulder. "Hey, Claire."

Turning around, she smiles. "Hey, Ally, I haven't seen you for ages, where have you been?"

"Working in New York for Rufus Granger."

Claire's eyes widen. "I forgot you landed that one. Well, what was it like?"

The blush to her cheeks tells Claire what she wants to know, and she laughs softly. "I heard he was gorgeous. You didn't um…"

Shaking her head, Ally says in a shocked voice, "Good God, no, but I wouldn't have said no if he asked."

They giggle like school girls, and I strain to hear every word. Ally sighs wistfully. "To be honest, I would have stayed if I could, but my visa ran out. You know, Claire, New York is such a vibrant place to work and the guys are well…"

She fans her face and Claire raises her eyes. "Go on."

Ally giggles adorably. "Well, put it this way, I was in demand in more ways than one. Anyway, I'm back working on boring hedge funds and tearing my hair out, waiting until I can apply for my visa again. What about you, what's going on, I heard you were leaving?"

By now they've reached the front of the line and I say brightly, "May I take your order?"

Claire orders her usual and says kindly, "And whatever my friend is having."

"Oh, thanks, I'll have a skinny latte please."

I turn to make their drinks slowly, hoping they pick up where they left off and Ally says, "I heard you're leaving, anywhere I should know about."

Claire laughs. "Scott has a new job in Bermuda and we're heading out there for six months. It's all tax free and I don't have to work. How that's for a result?"

She grins and Ally looks green with envy. "You're so lucky. Not only have you snagged the most eligible bachelor in Canary Wharf, he's now whisking you away to paradise. Some girls have all the luck."

Claire smiles smugly and then my blood runs cold as she says lightly, "If you like, I'll put in a good word with Julian. He's pissed I'm leaving and if I tell him I've found the perfect replacement, he may actually be civil to me for five minutes."

Ally looks at her eagerly and my heart sinks. This is a disaster.

They move away and I feel agitated. What was I thinking? I'm no match for these women. They could do this job standing on the well-styled heads. I'm just a waitress and a cleaner. Why on earth would I be chosen above them?

Leah looks over and says with concern, "Are you ok, honey. You've turned a strange colour."

"It's fine, maybe I just need to eat something." I smile quickly and try to bring my head back in the game and she shakes her head. "You've been working for hours. Go and grab five minutes, I can hold the fort. Hailey's just arrived, so why don't you take a break?"

I know it's against the rules; none of us can skip the lunchtime rush, but I am grateful for five minutes to sort my head out, so I smile gratefully. "Thanks, I'll just take a comfort break, I won't be long."

I head off and shut myself in the ladies and try to unscramble my brain. My heart starts to slow a little as I try to calm down. Taking a few deep breaths, I give myself a stern talking to and try to think of a way out of an increasingly bad situation. I need to be clever about this. I can do this; I just need to work out how.

Five minutes is all it takes to get my head back in the game. Yes, I can't afford to falter because the stakes are too high. I will just need to rise above my competition, and I think I know just how I'm going to do it.

4

When I wake the next morning, the irritation wakes with me. I can't believe I was so unlucky yesterday. As soon as I stepped foot inside Crossline, my supervisor cornered me and thrust a new recruit under my nose. She shadowed me for the whole evening and I was unable to gather any information at all. Lisa, as usual, disappeared off to the executive floor and I was beyond frustrated that I had to babysit a newbie.

To add to my irritation, this morning I'm not alone because it's Sunday and Ronnie's home.

He arrived home in the early hours and crawled into bed beside me. I have grown so accustomed to being alone at night, his presence is now unwelcome.

As I move, a hand shoots out and pulls me back and he murmurs, "Don't leave."

Immediately, I tense up because sex with Ronnie was not my priority today, but he is my husband and it's been a long time.

Inevitably we have sex as rarely as we speak these days and have settled into the role of cohabiters rather than husband and wife. However, today he appears in an amorous mood and as it's been so long, even my libido could use being shocked back to life.

As he kisses me deeply, I close my eyes and imagine a different mouth on mine. I see another man before me as I picture Julian Landon in my bed. The image makes me feel sexy and adventurous, and I find myself responding to a man who doesn't even know I exist.

As I pretend to make love to a man I could never attract in real life, I allow myself to be carried away to a world where my dreams live for most of the time. I am no longer making love to my husband, but the man I hope to call my boss one day. I imagine us locking his office door and indulging in the sins of the flesh during the working day. I groan as I picture his hard body on top of mine and imagine a time when everything is perfect with my life. However, before I even reach my own orgasm, Ronnie grunts and gets his own happy ending and rolls off, mumbling, "Sorry love, it's been so long I couldn't last."

Feeling slightly let down and a little frustrated, I just say reasonably, "It's fine, don't worry about it."

As he rolls over and reaches for his phone, I slip out of bed and into the bathroom.

Heading for the shower, I soap my disappointment away. I picture Julian touching my skin as I rub the lather over my body and picture him kissing me all over. As I allow the imagery to take hold, I finish what my husband started and bite my lip as I climax, picturing Julian Landon as the man who got me there.

As the water washes away my shame, I try and get a grip. What on earth is happening to me? I'm becoming obsessed and should end this fantasy here. But I can't. I need this. I need to reinvent myself and as I think about how I can, an unwelcome thought pops into my mind. I no longer love my husband and this could be my way out of a future so boring I can't cope.

As I towel myself dry, I feel on edge as I realise that this job has taken on an even greater importance. I need it to save my future because I can't take much more of this. I must get out for my own sanity, and that job is the key to my freedom.

As I make us breakfast, my mind goes into overdrive. What if I succeed? Would I really just walk away from my marriage – my life? It doesn't seem possible and yet, there's a spark of hope deep inside that refuses to die. It's as if I'm waking from a bad dream and everything that happened before is in the past. I feel so agitated because what if… what if I fail?

"It's bloody raining again, typical."

Ronnie's words bring me back to reality and I watch as he shuffles over to the table and flicks on the television. It's hard to believe we had sex just twenty minutes ago because the man sitting before me could be any old stranger from Barrington's. Like them, he doesn't even grace me with a friendly smile or an appreciative look. He takes what he wants and gets on with his day, and I've had enough. So, I don't even answer him and carry on frying eggs and trying to push down my anger. I deserve more than this; I always did. Why did I settle so quickly?

We eat in silence as usual, and I find myself focusing on the news instead of the man before me. Once again, they are talking about Brexit and I'm bored with it. I'll say one thing for the press. When they get a story, they run with it. It's no wonder the public are fed up with it. The press has milked this for all it's worth, and it's getting boring.

Like your marriage.

That nagging little voice inside my head won't go away and so I try to silence it by saying brightly, "Shall we go out today?"

Ronnie looks up in surprise and I stifle a giggle because he looks so astonished, I could have told him I was running for Prime Minister. "What... out? Out where exactly?"

"I don't know, maybe go for a walk, or head to the shops."

"A walk? Are you bloody mad? It's pissing down outside and you want to go for a walk? Honestly, Emma, you're losing it."

He carries on eating and I try again. "Well, ok, maybe a walk was a stupid suggestion but we should get out. Maybe have lunch somewhere; what about that pub in town that's just been refurbished? I've heard good things about that."

He shakes his head. "Who from?"

"What do you mean?"

"Who did you hear that from?"

I feel a little thrown and just stare at him in confusion and he rolls his eyes. "I said who did you hear that from because if my memory serves me correctly, you don't have anyone who would tell you about the 'nice new pub' in town. In fact, Emma, I can't remember when you last spoke to anyone who wasn't a customer, me included."

"What do you mean?" My voice sounds weak and incredulous even to my own ears and Ronnie laughs but it just sounds mocking and brutal as he snaps, "You are so wrapped up in your own little world, you don't see half of what's going on around you. We never speak, we never touch, and we never communicate in any way at all. I work hard and I'll admit you do too, but we have zero to show for it. Why do we even bother because this isn't a marriage, it's a…"

He breaks off and pushes his plate away angrily.

"It's what, Ronnie?"

I'm not afraid of his answer, in fact I almost welcome it because maybe, like me, he has concluded that this marriage is a sham and wants out. This could be the best conversation we've had for years and so I hold my breath and wait for the final blow.

"I want us to have a baby."

I stare at him in shock and he nods. "We can't go on this way for much longer and need to inject new life into our marriage. I've been thinking about it for some time and the more I have, the more I've realised what's missing."

"A baby, are you mad?"

He looks angry and I feel the irritation reach boiling point inside me. "I thought you were going to ask for a divorce. I thought you had given up on our marriage and wanted out. I thought we were done and there was no going back and you want a baby! Are you mad?"

Ronnie's eyes narrow and he says icily, "Of course I want a baby, any sane person would. We are married for god's sake; it is what people do. They set up home and have a family, but not us. No, we've fallen into some sort of friendship couple because you are so bloody cold you freeze my balls off. So, yes, I want us to have a baby because that's obviously what's missing in our lives. You can give up work, we'll manage. I've been saving for some time now, so what's the point of money in the bank and working all the hours God sends to add to it. Now is our time, Emma. We need this, this life we lead, it's not normal. In fact, this whole set up isn't normal and you're deluded if you think it is."

He reaches across the table and takes my hand, lowering his voice. "I'm sorry, babe, I must take my share of the blame. I'm never here and have neglected you for a while. I want us to be a proper couple again. I want us to laugh and actually speak to each other. I want this home to be full of life, instead of just a place to come home to after work and rest before going back there. We need to shock this marriage back into life and what better way than adding another to it. What do you say Emma, shall we give this a go?"

As I stare at him, I am totally mesmerised because the sullen, whining husband I'm used to seeing, has been replaced by the boy I fell in love with. The years have just melted away and he is sitting before me offering me the promise of a new life full of excitement and shared dreams. I can't even form words because I'm back in a time when my life held promise and excitement. Could this be the solution to our problems? Do I want a baby – with him?

He kisses my hand and says gently, "I think you're right. Go and get glammed up and I'll take you out somewhere. The chores can wait for one day, we need to talk."

"But the dishes?"

He smiles. "I'll see to them. Decide on a place you want to go and I'll take you. Today is your day and nothing is too much trouble."

Nodding, I scrape back my chair and leave the room as if on autopilot. A date…with my husband? I should be ecstatic, but I'm not. I don't want to make conversation with him; I want to walk away to a bright new world. Then again, maybe I do owe him this last shot at saving something that once meant everything to me. Maybe he'll agree that a change is as good as a rest and support me in my change of career.

Feeling a little brighter, I head back to my room and select a different outfit for the day. Yes, Ronnie's right, we need to shake this marriage up – our lives up, but he's wrong about the solution to our problems. I don't need a baby, I need a career, not a job.

5

It feels strange being out on a date with Ronnie. I can't remember the last time we actually spent time together, which is shocking considering we're married.

He is surprising me today. There's something different about him that I can't put my finger on. I actually think he's listening to me and I'm feeling quite excited for the day ahead.

As we set off, he says cheerily, "I thought we could go to town and you can buy something nice. Then I'll treat you to lunch at that new pub you told me about earlier."

I feel a little wrong-footed and say softly, "What's going on?"

"What do you mean?"

"This… going out, buying me something; the lunch and the sex. What's really going on, Ronnie?"

He sighs and I regret saying anything as he says wearily, "I've been thinking a lot lately. It's quite lonely driving around town late at night, and it got me looking at our lives. When did things change for us because I can't remember the turning point?"

I fall silent because it appears he has been having much the same thoughts as me. Shrugging, I say in a whisper, "I don't know."

"The thing is, Emma, I don't think I know you anymore. We hardly spend any time together, and that's not good. I drive couples around who actually talk and can you believe, laugh occasionally? Sometimes they even appear to enjoy each other's company and I want that – for us."

Every word he's saying is true and yet I worry that I've moved further apart than he has because it's not my marriage I'm intent on saving, it's my own future without him in it. Is there still time for us, or have I already given up? He deserves the chance at least, so I inject a little warmth in my voice and try to sound excited. "You're right; we need this day. I've been unhappy for a while now and something needs to change and this is a good start."

He looks happier and it feels good to see. Maybe I'm being a little too harsh on him. Everyone deserves a second chance, don't they?

By the time we arrive in town, we have reached a certain understanding. Today is the day we start trying. If it doesn't work out, then at least we gave it our best shot.

For the first time in absolutely ages, I go shopping with my husband. We wander in and out of the shops and he even grabs my hand on the odd occasion, which feels nice. He treats me to a pretty dress I admire on the mannequin in a dress shop window, and I actually laugh a couple of times at something he says. As the day progresses, it's as if we are walking out of a choking, oppressive fog. The man I fell in love with all those years ago appears to be still there, and soon I feel relaxed and easy around him and increasingly attracted to the man I married.

By the time we arrive at the pub for lunch, I am feeling quite upbeat about our future and from the look in his eyes, he feels the same. I even can't wait to return home and finish what we started earlier because this Ronnie is an attractive man, who I want to know again - intimately.

We are shown to a table by the window and as I peruse the menu, he says quickly, "Sorry, I need a call of nature. I won't be long. If the waiter comes, order me a steak and the usual beer."

He winks as he heads off and I smile. Yes, I married this man for a reason which is coming back to me now. Maybe it's not too late after all.

I make my own selection and look around with interest. The pub used to be quite dated but is under new management and they have refurbished it well. It's a lot more modern and up to date, and the furnishings are warm and comfortable. As I look around, I study the people sitting at the nearby tables and feel happy to be one of them for a change. The conversation is loud and there is much laughter. Couples, friends and families are all enjoying their lunch and suddenly Ronnie's suggestion of starting a family doesn't seem such a bad idea.

I see him walk back into the bar and my heart flutters. He was always an impressive looking man, dark hair cut close and deep velvet brown eyes that I used to lose my soul in. Six-foot-tall with a muscular body that hasn't changed. He works out and subsequently his body has developed into one he can be proud of and now, seeing him through an open pair of eyes, I feel the unfamiliar stirring of lust grip me hard.

I am slightly surprised when he doesn't head straight back and leans across the bar in conversation with the bartender. He can't see me looking and I notice the bartender point in the direction of the door at the end and Ronnie nods and heads in that direction. Maybe the restrooms are through there and he made a wrong turn? However, I see the arrow for the men's pointing back the way he came and I'm curious. If I lean slightly back, I can just about see through the open door and notice him heading to the far side and shuffle towards a table at the end. There is one person sitting there and I can see it's a woman. Straining to see, I watch as he slips into the seat opposite her and I can just about make out her expression. She looks wary.

Feeling extremely curious, I leave my seat and edge towards the door, making sure I'm hidden from view and pretend to be looking for something. I suppose I am because I see the woman's face clearly as she says something to him urgently, and even from here, I can tell she's upset. Ronnie is shaking his head and I see his fists balled tightly, which he always does when he's angry. The woman appears to be crying and goes to say something, but he stands and I scurry back to my chair, my heart hammering within me as I sense something isn't quite right.

Quickly, I sit back down and lift the glass of water to my lips as the waiter heads over.

"Are you ready to order, madam?"

Nodding like a fool, I say quickly, "Um, steak and fries and a bottle of Peroni please. I'll have fish and chips and a glass of house red, thank you."

As he notes down my order, Ronnie heads back and smiles. "Sorry about that. I had to wait longer than I thought. Have you ordered?"

The waiter reels off the order and he nods with satisfaction. "Perfect."

As the waiter heads off, Ronnie takes his seat and smiles. "Well, this is a rare treat, isn't it?"

I nod but can't form words as I struggle to ask what's at the forefront of my mind. I take a sip of water as he looks around and smiles. "This place looks much better. It was a good idea to come here."

My throat feels dry and there is something beating me up inside. It's the knowledge he isn't going to say a word about what just happened, which makes me wonder why. I quickly glance over at the table in the next room and notice the woman staring at us with a frozen expression. Something about her unnerves me and it must show on my face because Ronnie follows my gaze and says, "What's the matter, babe, you look as if you've seen a ghost?"

I can't help it and blurt out, "Do you see that woman over there, do you know her?"

He doesn't miss a beat. "That's Caroline, Stuart's wife. Maybe he's around somewhere."

"Didn't she say?"

He looks surprised and a little on edge as I say bluntly, "I saw you talking to her."

If a flash of guilt shows in his expression, it's a fleeting one because he shrugs. "The barman told me she'd been there for two hours drinking solid. He asked if I was with her and I told him no, but I knew who she belonged to."

I stare at him incredulously. "Belonged to; are you kidding?"

"What, I'm just joking?"

He looks across at the woman and sighs. "Poor love, she's a bit deranged. It's due to her drinking problem. Stuart doesn't know what to do for the best, maybe I should call him."

He whips out his phone and I watch as he dials the number and says loudly, "Stu, it's Ronnie. Yes… um... ok… but that's not the reason I've called. Caroline's in the Blue Star; you know, the one by the iron bridge. I'm here with Emma and recognised her. You should get down here mate, it looks as if she's had a few already."

He nods and says quickly, "No problem, anytime. See you Thursday."

He cuts the call and I say in surprise, "Thursday?"

"Yes, the card game. Stuart's one of the club. It's at his house this week and I hope she's not around."

"Why?"

"Because Stu won't be able to concentrate if she is. You never know what mood she'll be in, and he's always on edge. Anyway…" He sighs and leans forward, taking my hand in his. "Let's not talk about them. I want to talk about us and our future."

I smile but don't really feel it inside. Ronnie may be a smooth talker with the gift of the gab, but I saw the look she gave him. It wasn't one that a wife would give her husband's friend; it was more than that. I'm not stupid, and judging from his reaction, I'd say he was a lot more familiar with Caroline than he's letting on. Suddenly, the date's been tainted and I feel anxious. Ronnie has a secret and I'm not sure I like the direction my mind is heading.

6

I am anxious to get to work on Monday. The weekend ended up to be a good one where Ronnie pulled out all the stops to reconnect us as a couple. We laughed, ate, drank and made love rather than the usual going through the motions. He was attentive and kind, which only made me suspicious because he did a complete one eighty on me and it's almost as if he's trying too hard.

However, I can't dwell on that now because I have more pressing business to deal with first. The job across the road.

As the day goes on, I listen hard for any sliver of information concerning it. Claire Quinn comes in as usual, but nobody speaks to her, so she offers no further update. I see Ally, the lady she spoke with before, frantically writing in a notebook which unnerves me because I guess she's prepping for an interview for the same job I want so badly.

As days go, it's an increasingly frustrating one and it's only when I change jobs and head across to Crossline, that my luck changes.

Declan Cole looks up as I sign in and I shiver inside. He may be good looking in a rough-and-ready sort of way, but he gives me the creeps. His eyes appear to strip me bare and leave me feeling filthy and violated, and I try not to look at him in the vain hope he will leave me alone.

"Hey, Emma, over here."

I cringe as I look up and nod. "Oh, hi, Declan."

He waves me over and reluctantly I head across and say quickly, "Is everything ok?"

He licks his lips and his dark eyes appear to penetrate my soul as he whispers, "You know, I really like you, Emma. We don't talk much and I wonder why."

I'm not sure what to say, so laugh nervously. "It's fine, you don't have to make conversation with me. I mean, usually that's reserved for Lisa, um… is she around by any chance?"

I look around for my friend, desperate for her to appear and distract the man who is setting my teeth on edge. He smirks and says in what I'm sure he considers a sexy voice, "Phoned in sick."

"That figures." I laugh softly. Lisa always has been a drama queen concerning her health.

He winks and says huskily, "You can clean the exec floor today. I've agreed it with your supervisor and the new girl Becky will do your usual offices."

He winks and says in a suggestive voice, "You can thank me later."

I can feel my cheeks are on fire as I mumble, "Ok, thanks, well, I should be going then."

Quickly, I head off and try to put as much distance between us as possible. I'm not sure why, but there is something so creepy about the flirtatious security guard and I can't put my finger on it.

However, unknowingly he has given me the opportunity I need at the right time. This is my chance to set my plan into action, and I can't waste a minute.

Grabbing my trolley, I head to the bank of executive elevators and wait impatiently for them to arrive. I know exactly what needs to be done, and I don't have long.

As soon as I step out of the lift, I sense the difference. It's much calmer, warmer, and oozes wealth. There is an expensive wool carpet stretching along the hallway and the corporate colours of navy and gold are everywhere, from the plush seating and insignia stamped on just about everything. The air feels different up here. Cleaner, fresher and filled with ambition. Power lives on this floor and the walnut panelling and wooden doors are in direct contrast to the standard issue one's downstairs.

As if in a dream, I wander through the offices, for once speechless as I take it all in. Polished wooden desks, hold brass desk lamps and padded chairs are pulled neatly against the large, paper free desks with nothing but leather-bound ink blotters in residence. Silver photo frames are home to photographs of glamorous looking families, and well-watered pot plants convert the CO_2 to oxygen in the room for the inhabitants to feed off.

I wander around in awe until I remember why I'm here, so I head towards the offices of the head of human resources where my task begins.

Harriet Masters is the head of HR and will be the woman responsible for selecting the final applicants. The first thing I do is sift through her waste paper bin to see if I can find anything to help me. Aside from the usual rubbish they throw away, I see her scribbles on white sheets of paper and fold them up to be studied later at home. Quickly, I grab a single sheet of paper and head across to her ink blotter and grabbing a pencil shade over the blotter revealing the indentations below. Once again, I fold up the paper and place it in my pocket.

Grabbing my polish and duster, I clean her desk, paying particular attention to the drawer fronts. Sliding each one of them open, I search for any notebooks or items that may be home to passwords or keys to the filing cabinets.

Quickly, I check her in-tray and see several unopened letters and as I turn my attention to the filing cabinet, I look around furtively before opening the top drawer and searching for the folder I am sure is here.

It doesn't take long and I soon find what I want. A folder marked Mr Landon's pa - applicants.

Quickly, I whip out my phone and take a photograph of every sheet of paper and then make sure I place them back where I found them.

Then I quickly tidy the office, making sure to do my job well because I will need further access to this floor.

As I move from office to office, I conduct the same search. It will pay me to know every detail of what goes on here and outside of the computer files that will remain private, I need to know about the people who work here.

By the time I reach the office of the one who interests me the most, time has moved on and I'm running late. Quickly, I head inside and look around in awe and disbelief at the offices of the man in charge.

Every bit as impressive as the others, but a hundred times more so. This room is huge and could be mistaken as the seat of power because it is just as I imagine the oval office or 10 Downing Street to be.

All around me is wealth, from the paintings on the wall, to the cut-glass decanters and matching glasses set beside a small off-licence of spirits. A comfortable couch sits to one side in front of a giant television screen. The window is panoramic and if it wasn't dark, I guess I would see the whole of London spread out beneath me. My heart beats faster as I look at the silver photos staring at me from the highly polished desk. Moving across, I see the man himself looking out at me with his arm slung around the shoulders of an obvious supermodel. Standing before them are two gorgeous little girls who look to be around 5 or 6 and are the spitting image of their glamourous mother.

I can't drag my eyes from the man I aspire to work for. I heard he was attractive, but this man is handsome. So handsome, from his dark slick hair and electric blue eyes, that are flashing as he smiles for the camera. He appears lithe and athletic, and his body strains against the polo shirt he is wearing tucked into beige chinos. His clothes look expensive and the surroundings are the grandest I have ever seen. His wife is, as I would expect, beautiful with a femininity that only the rich wear well. She is manicured and perfection personified, and her clothes wouldn't look out of place in a magazine spread in Vogue. I'm guessing their children go to private school and no doubt have a stable of ponies. This world they inhabit is intoxicating, and I want it more than life itself. This photograph, these offices, have fuelled my resolve. I must get this job; my life depends on it.

I am so engrossed in what I see before me, I am surprised to hear, "There you are. I'll take that thanks you owe me now."

7

"What?"

I take a step back because I wasn't expecting this. Declan has this look in his eye I don't care for, and I'm suddenly extremely aware of my vulnerable position.

He saunters into the office and closes the door softly, and my heart leaps as he turns the lock and removes his jacket.

"I've been watching you."

"Excuse me."

My voice sounds weak and feeble and my legs are trembling, threatening to give out on me at any time.

He removes his tie and says darkly, "On the monitor. I've watched you move from room to room looking at things you shouldn't. What's your story, beautiful lady?"

My head roars and I berate myself for being so incredibly careless. Of course, the CCTV - the cameras. It's what they're there for. To record and ensure the safety of everyone inside. How could I be so stupid?

He smiles creepily and grunts, "I said, I'll take that thanks now."

Quickly, I try to think of a way out of this situation and decide to play dumb. "Um... thanks."

I move to the other side of the desk and he laughs, a low hollow sound that has no humour in it.

"I want you to demonstrate how thankful you are. You see, as I see it, you have two choices. Do what I say and I'll keep your little secret, or you can refuse me and you'll never step foot inside this building again. Your choice, darlin', now what's it to be?"

He grins, sure that he has this all worked out and from where he's standing, he has.

"What do you want?"

He smirks. "Isn't it obvious?"

"No."

He laughs softly. "It's ok, darlin', I don't want to hurt you. Just fool around a little like Lisa does. She knows how to keep a man on side and you'll find the rewards are great. Take you, for instance."

"Me?"

"Your little search and steal you got going on there. I'm guessing you are looking for something and it's not above board. To be honest, I couldn't care less what it is, each to their own, but you see, if I keep your secret, you've got to reward me somehow. If you don't, I'll report you for snooping and your ass will be out of here quicker than you can shout rape."

"Rape." I feel sick to my stomach as he unzips his trousers and takes his penis in his hands. "I only want you to give me a blow job. A small price to pay for my silence, wouldn't you say?"

I feel sick and dirty and backed into a corner, and I'm not sure what I can do about this. The last thing I want is to be anywhere near the vile creature before me, and I feel the bile rising in my throat. Playing for time, I say softly, "I'll need a minute."

I see the excitement flash in his eyes as he strokes himself, groaning with anticipation. Spying a paperweight on the desk, I seize my chance and say huskily, "Go and lie on the couch, you'll be more comfortable there."

He licks his lips and growls. "Fuck, baby, you know how to turn a man on. Don't be long, I've only got ten minutes before I have to check in."

Feeling light headed, I just nod and smile sexily, "I'll be quick."

As he makes towards the couch, I back up to the wall and as I do so, drive the paperweight through the glass surrounding the fire alarm. As it shatters, the loud bell that starts ringing drowns out the sound and Declan jumps up shouting, "What the fuck?"

Frantically, he fastens his trousers and races for the door, shouting, "I need to get back to my desk and coordinate this. What the fuck is going on?"

I stifle a laugh as he runs wildly from the office, still oblivious to the fact it was me who set the alarm off in the first place.

However, my laughter soon fades as I realise what a hole I'm now in. Declan knows. He knows I'm up to something and now has a hold over me that he's unlikely to relinquish. I'm not stupid and know that as soon as he gets over this latest hurdle, he'll be back to claim his revenge and it won't be pretty. No, I need to deal with the problem and I know just know how.

Quickly, I finish up before the fire officers come in search of the cause of the alarm and make my way downstairs. I have some homework to occupy my time and feel quite excited about what lies ahead.

As I reach my locker, I see Becky changing out of her overalls and smile. "How are you getting on?"

She shrugs and says in a tired voice. "It's ok I guess, but I never thought it would be so boring."

Laughing to myself, I nod sympathetically. "It can be. However, like most jobs, it's what you make it."

Thinking of all the information I've gathered; I smile to myself. Yes, this job is way more interesting than it is on face value because it gives me the cloak of invisibility to get what I want.

Grateful for the fact that Ronnie is working, after my supper I spread out the paperwork I took from Crossline and study the photographs I took on my phone. It makes for interesting reading. It appears they have six applicants of any worth for the job. Three internal ones and three from agencies they use. Harriet has discounted two of them and I read with interest the notes she's scribbled on post-it notes attached to the relevant application. One doesn't have the relevant experience which is a problem for me and one had bad references, also a problem for me. The four that remain are good candidates and I see that Ally and Sarah appear to be the front runners.

As I study their applications, I take notes of all the points they've raised that are good and make an outline of their layout. Then I reach for my laptop and type my own resume and covering letter, making sure to include everything they have and more. When it comes to experience, I amplify my assets and like all works of fiction, I make it bigger, bolder and almost unbelievable. I'm banking on her not actually reading a word I have written, but at least it's a small piece of cover should I need it.

It appears that the closing date is tomorrow and interviews are scheduled for early next week, so I have a little time at least. Making sure to email my application to the generic email provided, I hold my breath as I press send. There – no going back and my heart beats with an excitement that it hasn't done for quite some time now.

Can I really pull this off? If I do, the riches are worth the deception. If I don't, the worst thing that could happen is I never hear back from them. Thinking of a possible interview gives me anxiety because I'm pretty sure they will see through me in an instant. Let's just hope it doesn't get that far.

8

The next day I almost can't concentrate on my work at Barrington's. Every time someone comes in from Crossline, I listen for any news that could help me, but today is obviously a slow news day and I feel increasingly frustrated as the day goes on. I see both Ally and Sarah and size up my competition and find myself lacking in every department.

Luckily, the day is routine and nothing gets in my way as I head to Crossline for my evening shift. Today I have something I need to do and it will take a miracle to pull this one off.

I breathe a sigh of relief as I see Lisa heading my way as I change and she pulls a face.

"Ugh, I can't believe I'm back here already. You know, having that day off really made me think."

"What about?"

"This - my life. You know, Emma, I'm not like you - I want more. I mean, it's ok for you, you have a husband and a home and have it all worked out. I'm still young with it all still to play for and this isn't how I imagined my life to pan out."

Far from feeling annoyed at her comments, I just smile. "What are you thinking?"

"Well…" She grabs her overalls and says with some excitement. "I've applied to work in one of the big stores in Oxford Street. My cousin works there and can't speak highly enough about it. I think

I stand a good chance, so if I'm suddenly gone one evening, you'll know I was successful."

She busies herself with her preparations and I smile to myself. I hope she gets what she wants because nobody should settle for second best, no matter how old they are. Maybe the wind of change has blown through both our lives and this time next year, we will be on a very different path.

It's with some trepidation that I head off to grab my trolley and start my shift. Now Lisa's back she will clean the executive offices, which makes things more difficult. I try not to look at Declan as I make my way towards the elevators and yet I can see his reflection in the shiny steel walls and my hearts settles as I see him deep in flirtatious conversation with Lisa. She is laughing and doesn't appear to harbour the same disgust that I have for him, and I feel a frisson of excitement as I think that my plan might just work.

I consult my watch and note that I have approximately two hours, so I work as if I'm possessed. I clean those offices like a robot and hardly stop to draw breath. Then, just before seven thirty, I head back downstairs and my heart lifts as I see the front desk empty where Declan usually sits. I head across and make a big show of cleaning the surrounding area and steal a look at the monitors. Quickly, I flick them to the executive suite and see Declan and Lisa in Mr Landon's office. By the looks of it, they've just met up because I watch him close the door and lock it as she moves towards the couch. Propping my phone in front of the monitor, I set it to record, making sure to pause the CCTV in the executive offices, silently thanking my father for all those boring Saturdays spent helping him at work when he did this very job at the local department store. Who knew I would need that lesson for this purpose in my future?

Then I head to the elevator leading to the executive offices. My heart thumps madly as I will the lift to travel faster as it heads toward the office I need.

It doesn't take long and I don't waste any time and head toward Harriet's office, sure that I'm not being recorded this time and carefully open the door.

Quickly, I grab the post-it notes I carefully copied and place one on Sarah's application in my best imitation of Harriet's writing. If I feel bad about sabotaging her chances, it soon passes as I place my own application in the filing cabinet, with the post-it note that was once on her application now firmly on mine. My heart thumps as I realise what a chance I'm taking because I am relying on Harriet delegating the paperwork to her assistant who will follow her instructions to the letter.

As I quickly head downstairs, I pass Mr Landon's office and shiver as I think of what goes on in there at night. I wonder if he knows; he soon will if I get my chance?

By the time I reach the front desk, it has been all of ten minutes and I feel relieved when I grab my phone to see Declan pulling up his trousers and Lisa hastily rearranging her clothes. Perfect, job done. Just the insurance I need should he come looking for me.

Making sure to stow my trolley, I think about the next stage of my plan. This one will be riskier, but the adrenalin now shooting through my body makes it far more exciting than scary. Once again, I don't have long to prepare, so without waiting a minute longer, I head home for the night.

The next morning, for the first time since I started working there, I call in sick. I feel a little bad because it does leave them in the lurch, but that can't be helped. I need the day to execute my plan and I don't have long.

Taking extra care with my appearance, I shower, style my hair and apply the make-up that totally transforms me into one of them. The people I aspire to be like in every way possible.

Then I gather my folder and head towards the town, intent on picking up a smart suit to make me look the part in every way.

I know what I'm planning is risky to the extreme. For all I know, Mr Landon will be angry and have me thrown out onto the street where I belong. However, I have to try because there is no doubt in my mind, I won't get this job through the normal channels, so I polish my resolve and straighten my back as I set off to battle.

Two hours later and my own mother wouldn't recognise me. I certainly look the part and on face value I am every bit as competent as the other applicants. However, I lack the basic experience needed for this position, which theoretically should dismiss me out of hand. However, I can't let a minor detail like that get in my way, so I head to the coffee shop on the other side of Crossline Wealth Management and do what my own customers do every day – I order a coffee to go.

However, this coffee is not for me and I laugh as it strikes me that coffee may well be part of my success. Fingers crossed, anyway.

As I walk the short distance to Crossline, I hold my security pass gingerly in my pocket and take a deep breath. I can do this; it just takes courage and lot of bravado.

As I reach the reception, I am pleased to see that Declan isn't on the day shift. I'm not sure why I thought he would be, but knowing my luck he swapped with someone. However, the man that sits in his chair is a different one and doesn't give me a second look as I march past him with my lanyard swinging confidently as I walk. I don't stop to make conversation, or eye contact for that matter, and just stride towards the executive elevators as if I have every right to.

Nervously, I wait for the lift and try to control my beating heart. I can do this; I just know I can and as the lift arrives, I swallow hard and step inside along with five other people.

If I thought they may challenge me, I was mistaken because these people don't give me a second look. They stare at the ceiling, the walls, or the ground, and fumble with their phones with an air of boredom I can't understand. This is the dream – surely. Why wouldn't they be beaming around and congratulating themselves on making it? I'll never understand people. Do they realise just how lucky they are?

The lift arrives at its destination and I join the crowd of people streaming down the hall. As I walk, I tell myself I have every right to be here and nothing will stand in my way. In no time I reach the executive suite of offices that Julian Landon occupies and I slow for just a fraction of a second. What was I thinking?

Now I'm here, my resolve is in danger of crumbling. Am I really that naïve to think Claire will let me just breeze into Mr Landon's office without an appointment? I can see her head bowed to her computer as she concentrates on her work and the nerves almost make me change my mind and I step inside an empty room and take a deep breath.

Now I'm here, I'm not so sure this was such a good idea. The trouble is, my application may not pass scrutiny, and if Harriet Masters is anything to go by, I'm almost sure of it. Thinking of Ronnie and the direction my life is heading makes my resolve harden. I'm better than that. I deserve more. I'm not ready to give up work and be a mother before I've even tried to see if I've got what it takes.

Gripping the takeaway coffee more tightly, I toss back my head, straighten my back and head purposefully toward Julian Landon's office.

9

"May I help you?"

Claire Quinn looks up with a curious smile and I say brazenly.

"Mr Landon called down and requested a coffee. He asked me to deliver it personally."

Claire looks surprised. "Are you sure, it's just that I always get his coffee. Maybe it was someone else."

"No, he gave strict instructions that I was to bring it to him, personally."

I lean down and whisper, "I'm sorry Miss Quinn, but this is rather a delicate matter. The coffee is just an excuse, he um…"

I see the shock in Claire's eyes as she takes the bait and I undo a button on my shirt and wink.

Looking slightly flustered, she says, "I'll ring through, um… take a seat Miss…"

Shaking my head, I whisper, "I wouldn't do that if I were you."

"Why not?" A hint of steel creeps into her voice as she senses a challenge and doesn't like it.

Lowering my voice to a whisper, I say, "His wife sent me. It's a surprise from her to him. You know these rich types, more money than sense. He won't like that you know. Just let me pass and I'll say I sneaked in when you were in the ladies. He won't be angry; I can guarantee that."

She still looks unsure. "I'm sorry, I'm just not comfortable with this."

I nod towards my pass and say softly, "She even had this made up to ease my way in. No questions asked and no explanations needed. I'll be thirty minutes tops and then be on my way. He need never know of our conversation."

I can see her weighing up the situation and after a while says with resignation, "Oh fuck it, it's not as if I care, anyway. I'm off to pastures new and the kinky git can do whatever he wants. It won't be the first time, after all."

Now it's my turn to be surprised as she stands and whispers, "I'll be gone five minutes. Good luck, you're going to need it."

I watch her head off and stare after her in surprise. Well, that was easy. Maybe Mr Landon has a few secrets of his own that nobody knows about.

However, I don't have time to dwell on that and feel a little weak as I head towards his office door.

Knocking gently, I hear a deep voice shout, "Come in."

As I edge inside, the scent of an intoxicating aftershave greets me and makes my mouth water. I look across to the desk and see the man himself and my mouth goes dry. Wow. He hasn't looked up yet, probably thinking it's Claire and I take a moment to study him.

Julian Landon is the most impressive man I think I have ever seen. He exudes power and he hasn't even looked my way. He's wearing a starched blue and white striped shirt rolled up to his elbows. His tie is loose around his neck and the top button is undone, showing the hint of a tanned body beneath it. His forearms look muscular with a smattering of dark hair covering them, and his jawline is carved from granite as he frowns at something on his computer screen.

As I stare at him, I feel the desire sweep through my entire body. What would it be like with a man like him?

Then he looks up and I find myself staring into two pools of velvet brown, liquid desire. He looks curious but not angry which gives me the courage to stride forward offering the cup.

"Mr Landon, I apologise for the interruption, but I have a proposition for you." The silence is awkward to say the least, so I set the coffee before him and say in my most efficient voice, "Espresso, double shot, double boiled, just the way you like it."

He stares at me in utter disbelief as I stand inwardly shaking before him. On the outside I present the cool, calm exterior of a woman who does what she wants, when she wants, which is in direct contrast to how I'm feeling inside.

Then he speaks. "I'm sorry, did we have an appointment?"

"No, sir."

"Then how have got past security and then past Claire?"

He sounds curious, not angry and I say firmly, "I lied my way inside."

Leaning back, he studies me for a moment and then reaches for the coffee, takes a sip and I relish the pleasure in his eyes as he savours the flavour of his favourite drink.

"You have done your homework."

"Yes sir, in more ways than one."

He nods towards the seat in front of his desk and says firmly, "Sit."

I do as he asks and feel a little unnerved by the way he is openly staring at me. I see his gaze travel the length of me, lingering on my exposed cleavage, and see the flash of something that can only be described as desire spark in his eyes. Playing up to his interest, I lean back and cross my legs and say softly, "I am here to offer my services as your new assistant."

He looks at me in total shock and I say quickly, "Please allow me to explain my unorthodox behaviour, Mr Landon. All I want is five minutes of your time to persuade you I am what you need."

Nodding, he leans back and sips his coffee and then says, "You have until the cup is empty."

As the opportunity opens up, I say quickly, "I am unlikely to make it to interview through the usual channels. I have no experience and no references." He says nothing but I see the light die a little in his eyes and then spark again as I say, "But I'm good at what I do and I have discovered many failings in your operation that I'm happy to share with you."

"Such as." His tone is even, but I sense the storm in his eyes and I take a deep breath.

"Firstly, I know that one of the applicants, Ally Morris, has applied purely as an interim measure. She is currently waiting to return to New York where she feels happiest, but her visa has run out. Sarah Stammers, another front runner, is currently working here as a temp. She likes to gossip and is always chatting about the managers she works for pointing out all their flaws. For example, I know that Fenella Sullivan is planning on resigning because her boss is intimidating her and bullies her every hour of the day. She is currently building a case for the tribunal she intends on putting your company through for bullying in the workplace and anything else she can throw at you.

Her boss, Miles Sinclair, is an oily piece of filth whose main ambition is to make it upstairs to the executive offices. He is currently pursuing Alice Vander Woods, who is the HR managers assistant, to ease his way in. The fact he is married with two children doesn't stop him from having an affair with Alice to get what he wants. I also know that when the offices are closed your security guard likes to screw the cleaner on that very couch over there."

I point to the couch and see his eyes widen in disbelief. Warming to my subject, I say confidently, "I also know that your staff are unhappy and are free with their condemnation in public places where your competitors can listen to every word. I know that you are a very demanding boss and are considered ruthless and unapproachable. You see, I know a lot of things that passes the average person by. I study people, Mr Landon, and have an eagerness to learn. If you give me the chance, I will work 24/7. I'll give it everything I've got so you never regret hiring me. I want you to look back on this meeting as the day you met your best ever assistant and I want to prove that you were right to give me the chance."

Leaning forward, I make sure he gets an eyeful of my cleavage as I lower my voice and say softly, "All I ask is for an interview along with everyone else. Will you give me that shot at least?"

He sets the coffee down and says in an emotionless voice, "Finished."

I stare at him as he studies me and can see his mind working hard as he contemplates what I've said.

Reaching inside my bag, I place my application on his desk and say calmly, "My application, sir. I hope this isn't as far as it goes."

I make to stand and he barks, "Sit!"

My heart thumps so hard I'm sure he can hear it as he leans forward and says roughly, "Firstly, I don't like to be played Miss…" he looks down. "Sorry, Mrs Carter. Secondly, I don't appreciate you making my staff look like fools in front of me and thirdly what makes you think I am interested in someone as devious as you obviously are working for me?"

I shrink under his hard stare and feel my legs tremble as he says with tightly controlled fury. "You have overstepped the mark; Mrs Carter and you may think you have impressed me but it takes a lot more than that."

He taps his fingers on the folder I gave him and then lifts the receiver on his desk and barks, "Claire. Get here now!"

He sounds angry and I shrink under the hard stare he throws me as I see the fury in his eyes. I've gone too far.

Claire enters looking embarrassed and he shouts, "How the fuck did you let this woman in?"

Claire stutters, "She said it was a surprise from your wife."

He looks at her in astonishment, "My wife, are you a fool, Claire? Did you really fall for that one, it's as old as the hills? I'm beginning to think your resignation was a timely one, because obviously you aren't cut out for the demands of this particular job. You're a disgrace, Claire, a fucking disgrace and now get out of my sight before I have you escorted out of here by security with no reference."

Her face crumbles and she leaves, making me feel as if I'm the worst person in the world. Then he turns his fury to me and I cower under his gaze. "Mrs Carter, let me make myself crystal clear. I am not impressed by office gossip and neither do I give a fuck what my staff talk about during their day. I'd be a fool to think they thought any more of me than they do. I don't appreciate tales being told out of school and I demand honesty from my staff, which is something I doubt you have the capacity for. I don't need a spy, Mrs Carter, I need an assistant. Someone who can deal with the demands this job brings with it on a daily basis. Somebody trustworthy and keen to go that extra mile. Someone who can deal with my moods because I'm not an easy man to work for. You have zero experience by your own admission, so where would that leave me? So, in answer to your question, Mrs Carter, why should I give you the time of day when you have absolutely nothing I want."

He stands and I feel sick as I see the beast I have prodded too hard with a very misguided stick. If he knew my real role here, he would explode with rage. However, I stand firm and stare at him with a frozen expression as he turns and says in an icy voice, "Now get out."

I say nothing more and just stand, straight-backed and as if I have every right to be here. Nodding, I say in an unwavering voice. "Thank you for your time, sir. It was a pleasure to meet you."

Turning, I walk to the door and feel my heart fall into the gutter where it lives most of the time. At least I tried.

I walk past Claire, who stares at me with hate flashing from her eyes. She says nothing and just watches me walk proudly away. I try not to cry, but it's hard to stem the flow because I failed. I went too far and now I'm right back where I started. I don't belong here, and I was a fool to think I would ever fit in.

As I wait for the lift, I contemplate taking the stairs because the sooner I get out of here the better. As it arrives, I step inside and as the doors close, someone shouts, "Hold the lift."

My heart sinks as a well-heeled shoe wedges itself in the door and an extremely smart woman almost falls inside, catching her breath. The doors close and she looks at me with interest and holds out her hand. "Harriet Masters, head of human resources, you must be Mrs Carter."

I stare at her in surprise and my heart sinks as I shake her hand. "I'm sorry, I won't trouble you again."

She looks surprised. "Well, that's odd because I've just had a call from Mr Landon himself, instructing me to set up an interview for you. I was a little taken aback because I couldn't recall your application, but my assistant must have dealt with it because I found it with the others. Anyway, he was most insistent that I arrange it and you couldn't leave until we spoke. How does Wednesday at 4pm suit you?"

I nod because I'm speechless and she says kindly, "Just bring yourself, nothing else. It will start off with a formal interview with me and my assistant, followed by one with the man himself. If you're successful, we would set the ball rolling to get you in asap before Claire leaves because there's a lot to hand over. So, are you still interested, Mrs Carter, can I mark you as attending?"

Once again, I just stare at her in disbelief and then find my voice from somewhere and say quickly, "Of course, yes, thank you, I would be honoured."

Her eyes widen and I say quickly, "Well, maybe not honoured but happy to attend. Thank you so much, I am so grateful."

The lift arrives at the ground floor and she smiles politely and holds out her hand. "Until Wednesday, Mrs Carter, oh and Mr Landon asked me to tell you…"

I look at her sharply and she says with surprise, "He said he expects a lot more proof that you are what he's looking for and in greater depth."

She laughs softly. "I'm sure you know what he means, but I sure as hell don't. That man is an enigma most of the time anyway, but he's usually right. So, have a safe journey home Mrs Carter and good luck."

As I walk away, I'm smiling. Well, that turned out better than expected and I know exactly what preparation he is asking me for and luckily, it's just the type of thing I excel at.

10

I'm unsure whether to tell Ronnie or not but decide I should, after all, he will soon find out if I get the job, so he may as well be prepared. Ever since our date weekend, things have been a little less cold between us. We are still strangers that share the same house and work different hours, but occasionally he calls in the day and we chat like we used to. However, this weekend he says he has a huge surprise for me and I am excited to see what.

This weekend when we wake on one of those rare mornings together, he doesn't reach for me as I make to leave the bed. This time he leaves before I wake and when I do it's to the sight of him placing a tray of toast and jam with some heated croissants and a pot of coffee onto the bed. I blink as if I'm still dreaming and he smiles. "Morning gorgeous. I said I had a surprise for you."

Sitting back against the pillows, I smile. "This is amazing, thank you. I can't remember when I last had breakfast in bed."

He sits beside me and offers me some coffee and winks. "I thought of offering you something else but thought we'd start with food."

Giggling, I take a bite of the hot toast and groan. "This is good - seriously good. You're wasted as a cabbie, darling."

I'm not sure why, but he looks away and I wonder what I said. Then he clears his throat and says quickly, "Anyway, eat up while I tell you my second surprise."

I feel curious and he looks a little anxious. "I think we should move."

"Move, are you kidding, why?"

"Because." He shrugs.

"Because what; where is this even coming from?"

Sighing, he settles back against the pillows. "We're struggling in every way possible, Emma. Living here is hard work on the mind and pocket. It's so expensive everywhere and we are surrounded by people with a lot more money than we will ever have. I work nights in a job I hate and for what? There's no point to this anymore and if we want to start a family and actually have some money for once, we need to relocate to the north."

"What, North London?"

Rolling his eyes, he laughs softly, "You're a typical southerner, Emma. No, the North of England. I was thinking Lancashire. It's a lot cheaper there, and we could live like kings. I'd do some taxi driving, hopefully during the day, and with any luck you'll be a mum. We could afford a nice house up there because the rent's much cheaper. What do you say?"

I'm shocked and can't form words. The North of England. Why?

He leans across and rubs my shoulders. "I know it's a lot to take in, so think about it. I've approached a few letting agents and have a job lined up if I want it. I know it will be a massive change, but when you come to think of it, there's nothing keeping us here. Your family live in the Isle of Wight and mine, well… they aren't around anymore. Your sister can't stand us, and my brother keeps himself to himself. We don't have any friends to miss, so it's the best call we could make. What do you think?"

I feel faint. "I don't want to move." I say it slowly at first because I haven't really thought about it – it's quite a shock really, but that was the first thing that came from my mouth. As the news sinks in, I want it even less and say desperately, "But I've applied for a new job with more money, in the city. That could be the turning point we need."

Ronnie looks at me sharply. "Since when?"
"Since a couple of days ago. I was going to keep it as a surprise until I actually got it. The interview's on Wednesday."

Far from looking pleased as I would expect, he looks quite annoyed. "No."

"What do you mean, no?"

"As I said, if you start a new job, our family plans will have to take a back seat. Why start something when I've already thought of the best solution to our problems? I'm sorry Emma, but no, you can't take the job."

I feel the anger rising as I say roughly, "I'll do what I want. If I want the job, I'll take it."

Suddenly, Ronnie changes before my eyes and sweeps the tray of breakfast things to the ground and shouts angrily, "No fucking new job, that's an end to it. We're moving to Lancashire - end of conversation."

I stare at him in horror as he paces the room. "I can't believe you, Emma. You go behind my back and apply for something without consulting me first. How could you?"

My temper flares and I scream. "Says you, the man who's already got me packed and moving to god knows where without even a say in the matter. If anyone's being unreasonable, it's you, Ronnie. Why the rush anyway? We've only just started speaking again and here you are organising my life for me. No, I won't move because I kind of like my life here and if you don't, deal with it."

I know I've gone too far when he strides towards me and I see the rage in his eyes. I catch my breath because I've never seen him this angry before and his fists are balled tightly as he pushes me roughly back against the pillow. "You don't talk to me that way, never talk to me like that again or…"

"Or what, Ronnie? What will you do?"

I stare at him defiantly and he raises his fist to my face and I feel myself shaking as he growls, "Never mind what I'll do, just don't, ok. I'm sick of it. Sick of people thinking they can talk to me how they want. Sick of being dismissed as a nobody and talked down to if they bother to talk to me at all. Sick of being pushed around as if my life doesn't matter and sick of this bloody farce we call a marriage."

I feel myself shaking as I see the wild look in his eyes. He's on the edge and I never even knew. Then again, why would I, we never spend any time together, so how would I know?

I feel the tears building as he releases me and pushes me roughly back against the pillows. "Get dressed and clear this mess up. I'm going out."

I watch in disbelief as he reaches for the discarded clothes on the end of the bed and storms off to the bathroom and my hand flies to my throat as I sense the lucky escape I've just had. Ronnie has never been so physical before. It's as if he changed before my eyes and I don't like what he became.

It must be only ten minutes later that the door slams and I watch him jump in his cab and leave and I breathe a sigh of relief. Thank God. He's gone and the relief hits me hard. From nowhere the tears come, relentless and unstoppable as they drown my pillow with despair. What just happened? It all started so innocently and now look.

It takes me a while to piece together the events of the last hour and as I do, the anger returns. How dare he treat me like that? There's something very wrong with Ronnie and I have a dull ache where love once sat in my heart for the man I married all those years ago.

Move to Lancashire – with Ronnie. Not bloody likely.

11

Ronnie doesn't come back. In fact, Sunday passes, and every noise sets me on edge. The sound of a car driving past, or the crunch of gravel outside. A banging door, or a siren all make my senses tingle as I sense an approaching storm.

Even at night, I shake in my bed as I wait for him to return. However, as the hours tick by, it becomes apparent he's staying away and nobody is more pleased about that than me.

Monday morning comes and I watch the breakfast news with half of my attention. However, I look up in disbelief as they announce another missing person. A young woman who was reported to have never returned home after meeting a mystery man from the internet. This doesn't sound good and I watch as the presenter gravely tells the nation the details of yet another unsolved disappearance. There are four girls missing this year already and the police are treating them as linked and my mouth dries as I think about the prospect of a serial killer on the loose. All of the women come from London except for one from Oxford. It could be a coincidence, but by the looks on the faces of the presenters, they are fearing the worst.

Shivering with a sudden fear, I turn my attention to the job in hand. I need to gather as much information for Mr Landon as possible because he will want something so good, he won't have any choice but to hire me.

This time as I make my way into Barrington's, it's the owner Calvin Hunter who greets me. "Morning, Emma, it's a cold one today."

"Morning, where's Leah?"

"Called in sick. She thinks it's flu but you know her, she'll be right as rain tomorrow."

Feeling a little annoyed that I have to work with Calvin, I say sympathetically, "I hope she's ok."

He just grunts and sets about filling the coffee machine, and I turn my attention to the business of the day.

By the time mid-morning comes, I am so tired I need a break. There's a slight lull, so Calvin grants me ten minutes to grab a coffee and take the weight off my feet.

As I do, I surf the internet for the information I need and feel excited about what I may discover.

As I sit there in silence, a loud voice makes me listen. Two women are gossiping at a table nearby and one says, "Terrible about the missing girls. What do you think?"

"Sounds fishy to me. Nathan told me I'm not to walk on my own anywhere. He said it's the same man, he's sure of it."

Her friend gasps, "Really, oh my god, this is bad. I work nights at the Blue Star and always grab a cab home. What if it's a cab driver, I'm not safe?"

I say nothing and just stare ahead, a cold feeling washing through me like icy water, freezing my senses and planting images in my mind that have no reason being there. I can't shake the horrible feeling inside me as I picture Ronnie in his rage. Suddenly, every conversation we've had fills my mind and I picture the furtive looks and the uncomfortable silences as he hides something from me.

I feel sick as I think thoughts that should never enter my mind. I feel disgusted with myself for even entertaining the idea that my husband is somehow involved, but everything is adding up fast and I'm not prepared to face what it reveals. Could it be Ronnie – surely not?

I work as if on autopilot, and when Claire Quinn comes in, I feel a little worried that she will recognise me. However, my fears are unfounded because as usual nobody does. I am the grey woman to the grey man. Invisible and a mere presence, not an actual person. I walk in the shadows of other people's lives and have no life of my own to shout about. Nobody sees me because I shrink away into my own little world. I am a nothing, a nobody and the only words I hear are demands for my product or service. Is this what Ronnie feels like when he drives people around? Do they see him, I doubt it, we are cut from the same cloth and people like us don't draw attention to themselves? We have nothing to shout about anyway, so we listen. Watch and listen and move in the shadows where the invisible people live.

As I watch the workers from Crossline, I see a world I want to be a part of. I want conversation and shared lunches. I want to feel respected and valued and part of a team. I want the material things that come with the huge salary they earn, and I want to upload photos to Facebook of me in exotic locations. Surely it's not too much to ask – is it?

Calvin is nowhere near as much fun as Leah, and I'm glad when it's time to head across the road to Crossline. However, even that walk is filled with trepidation because of Declan Cole. I've been lucky so far, but I know it's just a matter of time before he settles up with me. I know he's angry, I haven't missed the fury in his eyes and the promise of revenge for setting off the fire alarm, which gave him a lot of paperwork to file and he had to be quick on his feet thinking up a reason why the alarm was broken in the first place.

No, I am on borrowed time as far as he's concerned and I approach the building with extreme caution.

However, it's not Declan sitting in his usual place, but a stranger. An older man who looks bored and surly. He looks up as I approach and nods as I wave my pass in front of him. I have to know and say timidly, "No Declan tonight."

His eyes narrow and he shakes his head. "Not tonight."

As I move past, I take with me a feeling of foreboding. Something's happened.

As I reach my locker, I see Becky stowing her handbag and she nods. "Hey, Emma. Have you heard?"

"Heard what?"

Once again, my heart thumps wildly inside me as I think I already know what her answer will be.

"Lisa's been fired along with Declan that creepy security guard."

She lowers her voice to a whisper. "Apparently they were caught on CCTV in an extremely compromising position. It's all around the building, can you believe it?"

Leaning against my locker, I say weakly, "I can't, poor Lisa."

Becky nods. "I heard she couldn't care less. Apparently, she was about to hand in her resignation, anyway. She told me last night she had a new job lined up in Selfridges. I'm not sure Declan is so happy, though."

"What makes you say that?"

"Well, my mum works in the canteen and she saw him get his marching orders. He was escorted out by security and everything. She heard him shout they hadn't seen the last of him and he wasn't going quietly. Can you imagine, I would have loved to see that."

I feel weak as I picture him angry and out for revenge. I just hope he didn't find out it was me who told on him because if that's the case, I should watch my back.

Becky carries on chatting, seemingly oblivious to any worries I may have. "So, Miriam told me I was on your floor and you're on exec. Lucky you, I'd kill to do that floor, it must be so nice to sift through the bins of the affluent."

She winks and heads off and I feel sick. It was one thing going up there as a job applicant, but now I'm returning in my usual role I'm not so brazen. What if they monitor the CCTV and see me cleaning the very offices I want to inhabit? I'm guessing I wouldn't get the job then.

However, I carry out my duties on autopilot as I think of ways to impress my hoped-for new boss. What would impress him? So far, I can't see how anything would, but he may be interested in some juicy titbit.

As I work, I plot and look for little nuggets of inspiration in every corner, on every surface and inside every waste paper bin on the executive floor.

Then my luck changes.

As I make my way out of the final room, I hear voices approaching. Quickly, I put my head down and push my trolley in the opposite direction but look in the mirrored glass of the office door to see who it is. I recognise Mr Slater, the man responsible for heading up asset management and a man I've never seen before. They are deep in conversation and don't even glance my way. I am invisible to them as usual, and for once I'm extremely glad of it.

They head into Mr Slater's office and I wonder what's going on. The man with him didn't look like the usual office worker, if anything, he looked a little shady. Maybe it was his dark European looks and casual clothes but it struck me as odd, anyway.

Moving to the office next door, I am aware they share a Jack and Jill bathroom. It's common in the executive offices, they have all the mod cons and I carefully push the door open and venture inside, hoping to hear their conversation without being discovered. I'm in luck as the door is open slightly and I hold my breath as I stand to the side behind the door and listen.

"Do you have the information I requested?"

The stranger speaks in a thick accent, and Mr Slater nods and slides an envelope across the desk. "It's all here, do you have my money?"

I watch as the stranger slides a similar envelope across and Mr Slater removes a piece of paper from it and smiles with satisfaction. "It's a pleasure doing business with you, Sergio. Remember, you never heard that from me."

I watch as Mr Slater pours them both a glass of what appears to brandy from the decanter on his desk and raises his glass in a toast. "To future business."

Sergio clinks his glass and says thickly, "The money has been deposited off shore as agreed. The trail leads to an investment company in Mexico and is so tied up in red tape, it would take a genius to unravel it."

Mr Slater laughs. "I hope so, for both our sakes. If Julian got wind of this, I'd be up on charges quicker than the deposit reaches my bank."

Sergio laughs and then stands. "I should go. It was risky coming here at all, but my man has assured me the files will be wiped."

Mr Slater nods. "We were lucky that fool of a security guard got fired today. It was the perfect opportunity to replace him with one of ours. You know, sometimes the safest place to hide is in the eye of the storm."

The men laugh and head towards the door and I feel my legs shaking with fear. What if they saw me? That was no normal business meeting, that's for sure.

I wait until I hear the lift ping and look at my stricken face in the mirror. If they see the CCTV, they will know I was here. What if their security guard saw me watching? I'm in danger and I'm not sure what to do about it. Luckily, the bathrooms have no cameras, but they would have seen that I was in here. I might get away with it but then again…

Suddenly, I don't feel so sure of myself, so I quickly gather my things and head for the lift. I need to get some distance between me and Crossline because this is all getting a little too hot to handle.

I make my way to my locker and quickly grab my things. I don't hang around because the sooner I'm safely at home the better.

12

When I get home, Ronnie is waiting.

My heart sinks as I anticipate another argument and as days go, this one is turning out to be one of a kind.

However, the Ronnie that's waiting is a different one to the man who left and he smiles his apology. "I'm sorry I lost my temper, babe. I don't know what came over me."

Throwing my bag on the counter, I say sadly, "You scared me, Ronnie."

He looks upset and I'm almost tempted to forgive him, but what would that achieve? So, I just reach for the kettle and sigh wearily. "The thing is, I don't feel as if I know you anymore. I don't think I know myself either. What's happening to us?"

He nods. "I agree."

His voice is soft and a little lost, and it strikes me just how far we've fallen as a couple.

Turning to face him, I smile weakly. "What's happening to us?"

He moves across and pulls me to his chest as he has a thousand times before. Then he strokes the back of my head gently and murmurs, "I love you, Emma."

Pulling back, I look at him in shock because I can't remember when I last heard him say those words. He smiles ruefully at my expression. "I do, I promise that at least, it's just that well…"

"Well what, Ronnie?"

I keep my voice low and even because I need us to talk. I must break down this barrier between us because it's destroying the people we once were.

"I'm sorry, the thing is, life hasn't exactly gone as I planned it."

"Do you want to talk about it?"

He pulls away and I immediately regret my words. I watch the shutters closing him down and he says lightly, "It's fine, nothing to tell really. Anyway, I came home to spend an evening with my wife for a change. Tell me about your day."

I swallow hard because what on earth can I say about my crazy day? Oh, I eavesdropped on a couple of men conducting a shady deal and will probably snitch on them to the man I want to be my new boss, or I got two people fired today because I ratted them out to the same man. I expect they will all now be out to get me and to top it all, I think you may be the man responsible for the disappearance of all those girls lately. Nothing much, same old.

Instead, I just shrug, "Nothing to tell really."

I quickly change the subject and reach for the fridge door. "Well, as you're home, maybe we can eat together for once. It's only sausages and oven chips, is that ok?"

He smiles a little wistfully and nods. "Perfect."

He pours me a glass of wine and grabs himself a beer and settles down in front of the television. As I prepare the basic meal, I watch him carefully. He looks normal enough; nothing like a man who would prey on women. I feel a little foolish for thinking it was him at all, but I can't drive the image from my mind about the woman in the pub. There was something so desperate about her and he was angry, I could tell. Are they having an affair, or is it something else? One thing's for sure, I appear to have lost sight of my husband and the same for him. We have grown apart and live like strangers.

As evenings go, it's a little frustrating. On the one hand, it's good to have some company and is almost like old times. Neither of us mention the reason for the argument, and I hope he's given up on the idea. Once I've washed the dishes, I snuggle down next to him on the sofa and we watch a thriller on the television. It feels nice doing such a normal thing because I can't remember when we last did.

Then we head off to bed and as he holds me tenderly in his arms, I feel the familiar feelings return that I thought were lost forever. Ronnie makes love to me so tenderly it makes my heart sing. Can we rescue our marriage, it certainly feels that way now? Only time will tell because one's things certain, I am going for that job and am definitely not moving to Lancashire.

Over the next few days, I get my head down and prepare for the interview and swot up on anything I think will help me. When I finish, I know Crossline Wealth Management like the back of my hand and have listened in on every conversation I can in

Barrington's and filtered every piece of waste from the offices that I stole. I've surfed the internet and made notes and consulted best interview practice, and if I'm not ready now, I never will be.

So, Wednesday comes and brings with it a lot of trepidation. To take my mind off it, I work in the morning pleading a dental appointment in the afternoon. I don't feel bad about lying because everyone does when they have an interview – don't they?

I brought my suit and make-up with me and make sure to head to a nearby hotel to get ready in their public conveniences. Then I sit in the coffee shop around the corner and mentally prepare myself. I can't let this opportunity go, it's become the most important thing in my life and I have a feeling that this job could change it forever.

So, at precisely 3.45, I head inside Crossline and walk purposefully towards the reception, just praying that nobody will recognise me in my smart suit with my hair down and styled properly.

I sign in and am instructed to take a seat in the reception area. Trying not to look anyone in the eye, I stare down at my notes and wonder if I've read this situation right. Digging up dirt goes against everything Mr Landon said to me and yet I'm not stupid, I know what was meant by his comment. He wants more, but is he prepared for what I'm about to say?

However, I need to get through Harriet Masters first and I smile as Alice Vander Woods heads towards me, smiling politely. "Emma, hi, I'm Alice, Harriet's assistant. Follow me."

I smile and, fighting the nerves, follow her to the elevators.

As we take the lift to the executive floor, she looks at me with interest. "You know, we were surprised by your application. Neither one of us remembers processing it but there it was hidden away in the file. I wonder who put it there?"

Willing myself not to blush, I smile and look puzzled. "Maybe a temp?"

She shakes her head. "No, it's just Harriet and myself. I suppose it could have been Claire. I mean, Mr Landon was very insistent you get the interview."

She smiles brightly as we reach the top floor. "Oh well, it doesn't matter how you got here, all that matters is you did. Now, don't worry, we don't bite but I can't say the same for Mr Landon."

She giggles and I decide I really like Alice. Thinking of her being used by the slippery Miles Sinclair makes my skin crawl. She deserves so much better than him and could probably have anyone she wanted. She's kind, pretty and intelligent. What on earth is she doing wasting her time on a creep like him?

I follow her to a meeting room where Harriet is waiting and she stands and shakes my hand, saying pleasantly, "Please take a seat, Emma."

Nervously, I sit facing them and Harriet looks down at my application with interest.

"So, tell me, Emma, why do you want this position?"

Taking a deep breath, I steel myself for the questions ahead and sit a little straighter, saying firmly, "Because I want to work for the best. I strive for perfection and want to offer my experience to a company I respect and admire. I want a career that allows me to put everything into and gain the satisfaction when I see what I do makes a difference. Crossline impresses me, as does all its employees. This is a place I could expand my horizons and hopefully make a difference to the lives of my employers. You see, I am at a crossroads in my life, Mrs Masters. I don't have children, or anyone to claim my time. I am married but between you and me, it doesn't look as if I will be for much longer."

They appear concerned and I smile. "It's fine, it's amicable and by mutual agreement, however, I want more. I want to see how far I can go without the chains of normal life holding me back. I am prepared to live, breathe and sleep this position and you would be hard pressed to find someone as committed as I am."

I stop to draw breath and they share a look. I can't read them and hope they don't see this as someone saying whatever they want to hear just to get a job because I meant every word. Even the part about my marriage because from the moment I stepped foot inside this building, I knew in my heart if there was a choice to be made between this or my marriage – this would win.

Harriet looks at my CV and says lightly, "It says here you worked for Gascon Industries as a pa to the chief executive, tell me about that role."

My heart is beating frantically because that is so far from the truth, if there was a lie detector anywhere near me it would be going mad right now. I put that in because the company went bust six months ago and there won't be any references required. I used to clean there in the evenings and know the people who work there and the general layout of the place, so can answer any questions with a certain familiarity. I then proceed to tell them exactly what I think they want to hear, and by the end of it, I've even convinced myself that I did the job.

I can see Alice writing notes and I wonder what they are thinking. Harriet continues to look at the CV and says with interest, "What did you do after Gascon?"

"I worked in a coffee shop because a friend of mine was desperate and as I was in between jobs, I helped out. When this opportunity came up, I saw it as a gift from God because I suppose I thought it had my name on it. I suppose you could say I was in the right place at the right time."

Harriet smiles, but her expression is unreadable.

For the next twenty minutes she explains the job in detail and asks me hypothetical questions to see how I'd react in certain circumstances. I believe I hold my own and breathe a sigh of relief when she wraps up the interview by saying, "Thank you for coming, Emma. If you have any questions at all regarding your application, feel free to contact Alice. Obviously, there are other applicants in the running and a final decision won't be made until early next week. If you are successful, we will notify you by phone followed up by a formal email. Do you have any further questions?"

"Not at the moment but if I think of any is it ok to email them?"

Harriet nods. "Of course. Now, as I mentioned before, you will leave us and meet Mr Landon for a second interview immediately. He has the final decision and it's important he gets to meet the applicants personally as he will be your direct boss. If you would like to take a seat outside, Claire will come and find you when he is free."

She stands and I take my cue and shake her outstretched hand. "Thank you so much for the opportunity, it was a pleasure to meet you."

She smiles and I turn to Alice and say the same, before following her to the door.

As I make to leave, Harriet says sweetly, "Good luck, Emma."

It's only when I take my seat that I wonder if she meant to wish me good luck in the job application, or for my interview with Julian Landon. Somehow, I think it was the latter.

13

He keeps me waiting for one hour and I sit silently fuming as I watch the workers going about their business all around me. Nobody looks at me, nobody comes to check on me, and nobody offers me so much as a glass of water.

When I first sat here, it wasn't long before Sarah left his office looking flushed and a little upset, if I'm honest. She looked at me and I saw the pity in her eyes as she hurried past. I'm guessing he wasn't so nice.

However, that was ages ago and nobody has been in since. Claire carries on working and doesn't even look at me and I can't blame her for that, after all, the last time we met I almost got her fired. That seems to be becoming a habit.

Then, just before 5 o'clock, Claire looks up and says in a dull voice, "You can go in now."

Immediately, she looks away and I feel bad. Great, she hates me. Not that I can blame her, but it's still not a nice feeling. I've always liked Claire and was impressed by the way she conducted herself in the coffee shop. She was always pleasant and set the bar high. I suppose I should be used to people not seeing me, but I thought it would change when I was one of them. Obviously not.

As I walk past her desk, something makes me hesitate and I stop and say awkwardly, "Um… I just want to say I'm sorry. You know... what happened the other day. It was wrong of me and I really didn't mean to get you in any trouble."

She doesn't even look up and snaps, "Don't keep him waiting."

Sighing inwardly, I turn and head towards his office, feeling like something that blew in from the gutter. Not the best start to probably the most important interview of my life.

Knocking loudly, I hear, "Come in."

As before, when I enter his office, Julian Landon is looking at his computer with a frown. Today he is wearing a white shirt and black suit and looks so incredibly attractive it makes my head spin.

For a moment, I stand awkwardly and then he says curtly, "Sit."

Like Claire, he doesn't even look up and I feel as worthless as I did a minute ago. Why are these people so rude?

For what seems like an eternity, he carries on with what he's doing and I wait, silently fuming on the inside. Do I really want to be like them?

Then he looks up and the sight of those deep, dark eyes, staring straight at me, makes me hold my breath for a second longer than I should.

"You're lucky I was in a good mood that day."

I say nothing and stare at him with a blank expression. He waits for an answer, but he can wait all year as far as I'm concerned because I have nothing to say in reply.

After a while, he nods and says irritably. "I still don't understand why you think you're a good match for me. On paper, you're a disgrace. I've read your file and the whole application should be tossed in the bin."

Still, I say nothing and stare at him with a frozen expression and his eyes flash as he says irritably, "Not so talkative now, are you? Well, tell me, Mrs Carter…" He leans forward and stares at me long and hard, "Why should I give you the job when someone much more qualified has sat in that seat before you?"

I try not to let his words affect me and shrug. "Because she wouldn't last five minutes."

"Excuse me."

"When she left this office, Mr Landon, which, may I add, was exactly 55 minutes ago, she looked upset. I'm guessing you weren't that kind to her and probably pushed her a little too far. If you employed her, she would hate every minute of it because I have seen first-hand how you treat your assistants. When I was last here, you tore Claire apart, which by the way was totally unprofessional of you. I'm guessing you need an assistant who will tell you straight when you're acting like a complete and utter asshole."

Just for a moment, he stares at me with a stunned expression and I say nothing but fix him with a look my disapproving mother would be proud of. He leans back and shakes his head and says softly, "Asshole?"

I nod. "Yes."

For a moment, I can't read his expression and think this could go one of two ways. Then he throws back his head and laughs loudly. "You know, Mrs Carter, God only knows why but I like you."

I breathe out.

"You see, I am surrounded by ass lickers all day long who tell me what I want to hear. They let me be the person I am because they are afraid to challenge me. You, on the other hand, you're not afraid of me and I like that. Yes, you want something from me but are not prepared to put up with shit just to get me on side. I like that in a person."

He looks down and says in a softer tone, "Emma."

Hearing my name on his lips feels nice and the way he is looking at me feels nice. It's a mixture of interest and incredulity, with a little surprise thrown in. All I can say in reply is, "Thank you, although I must just say for the record, I'm not sure if I like you Mr Landon. I'm afraid the jury's out on that one."

He laughs again, and now I have his full attention. "So, my little spy, what have you got for me?"

"Nothing."

He looks disappointed. "What do you mean, nothing? I thought I told you to do your homework?"

Taking a deep breath, I face him with a frozen expression. "I didn't say I hadn't done my homework but you see, the last time I gave you information you weren't interested. You made me feel stupid and as if I was telling tales to the teacher. Well, I value my information, Mr Landon, even if you don't and I will only tell you what I discovered if you ask me nicely."

I know I've gone too far when he brings his fist down on his desk and bellows, "Too far, Mrs Carter. Too far and too clever. I don't appreciate games and I asked you a question. You give me the information that shows me you're just what I need, or this interview is terminated. Understand one thing, Mrs Carter, I am the boss around here and I could tell you to stand on your head and sing, God Save the Queen, if I wanted to and you would do it. Do I make myself clear?"

Standing up, I throw him a withering look. "Then I bid you good day."

"What?"

He looks surprised and I shrug. "As I said, an asshole."

I turn away and say as an aside. "Oh, and just for the record, the information I have is something you really want to know. It's a shame you couldn't be a better man to hear it."

As I turn and walk away, I am shocked when he says softly, "I'm sorry, Emma."

I freeze on the spot and he says in a voice that is so soft, it's like the coolest whisper, "I apologise for my rudeness, please sit down and we will start again."

As I turn around, he stands and moves around the desk and walks towards me. Reaching out, he takes my hand and leads me to the chair which he holds out for me like a true gentleman. Then he kneels down before me and stares into my eyes, and I know I'm lost forever. My heart flutters out of control and my insides turn to liquid desire. This man is good, I'll give him that.

As he looks into my eyes, his own sparkle with promise and he says smoothly, "I like you, Emma. You intrigue me in a good way, and I don't think I've ever met anyone like you. Please excuse my earlier behaviour and accept my apology."

I nod as if in a trance and he smiles sweetly. "Now, we will start again. Mrs Carter, please will you be so kind as to tell me what you discovered."

He stands and moves back behind his desk and I breathe again. He is fixing me with a look that takes my breath away and refuses to give it back.

Stuttering, I know I can refuse this man nothing and say breathlessly, "Mr Slater."

His eyes narrow. "What about him?"

"He's ripping you off."

Now I have his full attention. "Go on."

His voice is tight and controlled, and yet his eyes tell a different story. There is a storm building, threatening to wreak havoc on anyone that gets in its way.

Taking a deep breath, I tell him what I saw and by the end of it, he brings his fist down on the table and snarls, "The bastard."

Looking down, I feel the tears building and feel broken inside. I can't believe I've become the sort of person who sneaks around in the shadows and tells tales on another to further my own career. I hate myself.

Then two hands grip my face and raise it to look at the man who I've discovered I love to hate. The storm has passed and he is looking at me with a mixture of awe and appreciation. He is so close I could just move slightly and feel his skin on mine and his breath is hot and sweet as he says, "Thank you."

Then he releases me and once again kneels before me, taking my hands in his. "Just so you know, Emma Carter…"

I lick my lips nervously and his eyes darken with a look I haven't seen in a long time – lust.

"You've got the job."

He walks back around his desk and takes his seat, before staring once again at the computer screen. Without looking up, he says briskly, "We'll be in touch, you may go."

Saying nothing, I stand and walk away on shaking legs. What just happened?

As I leave his office, it still hasn't registered that I did it. I actually went and did it. This is it; my new life starts now and it was all worthwhile. The lies, the deceit and the spying counted for something so fantastic in the end.

Claire doesn't look up as I pass, but I don't care. Her job is now my job, and I'm the one who made it happen.

Suddenly, the future looks bright and I couldn't care less how I got here anymore. All the matters is that I did and nothing can ever feel as good as the feeling that follows me out of Crossline. I'm ecstatic.

14

Ronnie's gone.

Call it a premonition, but I knew something was different as soon as I stepped foot inside the house. It *feels* different. As if all the life has left and I know immediately that my husband has left me.

Slowly, I walk into the kitchen where I see a white envelope on the countertop. My legs shake as I walk towards it and with trembling fingers tear it open and I stifle a sob as the words swim before my eyes.

I'm sorry, Emma. I tried, believe me I, tried but this has got too big for me to handle. I let you down and I'm sorry about that. I never meant to hurt you, but when the truth comes out, I know you will hate me and I deserve every bit of it.

I've left some money in the shoebox under the bed and there should be enough to keep you going for a few months. I know you will, but please don't hate me for what I did and just remember I always loved you.
Ronnie x

The letter falls to the floor and the tears join it. What does he mean? I stare into space as I try to comprehend his words. He's left me – really left me.

Then my worst fears come back to haunt me with a vengeance and I stifle a cry of terror as I whisper, "Ronnie, what have you done?"

On autopilot, I sit at the counter and just stare. What happened? Why has he gone, surely it can't be that bad?

It's the part of me that's a little relieved he's gone that hurts the most. Am I really that callous to feel happy he's made this easy on me? Then again, he is my husband and that has to count for something. I love him, surely, it's still there. The last few weeks have shown me the man I fell in love with alongside a man I don't recognise. It's the unpredictable side of him that scares me. The side I haven't seen until now, and the side that made up my mind I wanted out of this relationship. Ironically, he's done it for me and I should be happy – shouldn't I?

I don't think it really sinks in because I'm used to being here on my own. Then it hits me; I'll have to move out. I can't afford to stay here on my salary. Then again, perhaps I can. I've just secured an impressive pay rise, and maybe this was always going to happen. What if it was written in the stars and everything happens for a reason?

My thoughts rage out of control as I struggle to understand what this now means. It's too much to take in and a lot to deal with. Then I remember the shoe box waiting innocently upstairs. Maybe there's more than money inside and nestled among it are the answers I seek.

Quickly, I take the stairs two at a time and fumble for the box underneath the bed. As I pull it out, my heart beats fast and furious as I hope the answers lie inside.

As I lift the lid, I blink in amazement because there must be thousands of pounds in here. Bundles of cash, all bounded together in rubber bands. There are too many piles to count and I catch my breath. What is this? Why does he have so much money hidden away?

There are a lot of questions that need answers as I sit on the bed surrounded by the money. This can't be happening. Is it a dream? It certainly feels like it. Things like this don't happen to ordinary people like me; there must be some mistake.

As the night wears on, I think about everything and nothing. My thoughts are a jumbled mess that I don't think I'll ever sort out.

Somewhere in the middle of it though is a frisson of excitement burning brighter as the hours tick by. He's gone and my life changes from this moment on. I have money and a job and a whole new start in life. Will he ever come back – possibly? Then again, would I be happy to see him - possibly not?

As I lie back on the bed surrounded by more money than I have ever seen in my life, the overwhelming feeling I have is of – happiness.

However, soon the happiness is replaced by anger. Why has he left me? I deserve more than a Dear John letter left on the side. All of these years of marriage count for something, don't they? Suddenly, I want answers and it won't wait.

Quickly, I head to the wardrobe and rifle through the boxes inside. His clothes are gone, which causes the tears to fall once more. Seeing my own clothes hanging there next to an empty void reinforces the fact I'm now on my own. I don't deserve this, do I?

I find nothing inside the wardrobe, he's cleaned it out, so I turn my attention to the drawers. Once again, it's all gone and I bite back the scream that's not far away. There's nothing left. Nothing to say he was ever here in the first place. While I was sorting out my new life at Crossline, so was he. He was removing every trace of himself from my life and I want to know why.

I transfer my attention to the rest of the house and tear through it like a whirlwind. Drawers, cupboards, boxes and shelves are all searched methodically for one shred of evidence that he was here in the first place. Nothing. Nothing at all, which makes me even more anxious than before.

Grabbing my phone, I scroll to his number and call it. Why that's just occurred to me is a mystery because surely, it's the first thing I should have done? As the call connects, I merely get a recording telling me the number isn't recognised. This can't be right. Why would he change his number, it doesn't make sense?

Quickly, I search for his brother's number and as the phone rings, will him to answer it.

"Hi, Emma. This is a surprise."

The relief is overwhelming.

"Carl, thank goodness, have you heard from Ronnie?"

He sounds surprised. "Not for a few months. I think it was around Christmas, why what's happened?"

"I'm not sure, but he's left and taken everything with him. I've tried to call but his numbers not recognised, I'm so worried."

"Whoa, slow down, what do you mean, left?"

"Left, Clive, as in left me and taken all his stuff. He wrote me a note and told me he was sorry; sorry for what, I don't understand?"

I start to cry as the full force of what's happening hits me and Clive says urgently, "I'll be right over."

"What, from Cambridge? It will take hours. No, it's fine, stay where you are in case he turns up."

He laughs bitterly. "I doubt that, he's never been one to keep in touch."

I know he's right because Ronnie didn't get on with his brother. I never really understood why because Clive and Sarah have always been the kindest, nicest people you could meet. Come to think of it, Ronnie kept away from all his family and I never really understood why. I did ask him a few times and he just told me there was stuff in the past that couldn't be undone. I could tell it upset him so never really pressed the matter. Some wife I turned out to be. I never really took the time to find out why.

So, taking a deep breath, I say in as calm a voice as I can manage, "Just tell me if he gets in touch, please, Clive."

"Of course, you know I will."

"Even if he asks you not to tell me?"

There's a brief silence and I know I'm asking a lot, but then he says gruffly, "Even then. I can tell you're worried and I could batter him for doing this to you, it isn't right."

"No, it isn't but shit happens, you should know that."

Again, there's a brief silence and then he says softly, "If you need anything, and I mean anything, call me. I want to help."

The tears threaten to unravel me and I sniff, "Thank you."

I hang up before I totally embarrass myself, and then the grief hits me. My husband has left and something is very wrong. It must be so bad he's had to run from me, his wife and the only one who could help him.

Suddenly, I'm not so sure I want him gone after all. In fact, if he walked in that door now, I would be so happy I would forgive him anything – wouldn't I?

15

Two weeks later and there's still no word from Ronnie. I've tried everyone I know and come up blank. The most alarming thing I learned was that Ronnie hadn't worked at the taxi company for several months. They told me he had walked out one day and told them to stick their job. I felt foolish and couldn't get out of there quickly enough. Why didn't he tell me?

I tried to contact his friends who he played cards with but don't have their numbers. His company were no help with that either and aside from going to the police, there is nothing else I can do, I've reached a dead end.

As it became apparent I wasn't going to find him; I gave up. He obviously doesn't want to be found. So, I concentrated on my own life instead and prepared to start my new job by leaving my old one and making sure I had a wardrobe fit for my new role.

Now the day has arrived and I am due to start at Crossline as Julian Landon's personal assistant and I feel so nervous I'm not sure I will last the day.

This time as I walk into the building, it's to the job I always thought I deserved. A new life with the very people I admired from the shadows. Am I prepared to be recognised and known by name, or will I crave the anonymity the invisible people enjoy?

I sign in at reception, thankful the security guard is new and wouldn't recognise me. In fact, I doubt there is anyone in this building who would. I have been a part of their world for years, and yet they pass me in the street without a backward glance. Not anymore. No, now I'm someone important because I have the ear of the big boss himself and I can't wait to start.

Harriet meets me in reception and smiles. "It's good to see you, Emma. Are you looking forward to your new job?"

"I am, although a little nervous. I'm so grateful for the opportunity, though."

She laughs. "I'll have that in writing if I may, you may not be so thankful after a few days in Mr Landon's company. He's an acquired taste, that's for sure."

I feel a little bad for him as she bad mouths her boss and my disapproval must show on my face because she backtracks. "However, he's an impressive man who wouldn't be here now if he wasn't extremely clever and good at what he does. People like him need to be the way they are – driven and they are intolerant of the rest of the lowly workers who don't measure up to their standards."

Suddenly, she looks serious. "Measure up, Emma, because your life will be a lot easier if you do. Don't be complacent and discover how his mind works. Claire was a good judge of character and easy to get along with and even she struggled from time to time."

I smile gratefully. "Thank you, I'll bear that in mind. Um, about Claire, is she going to train me?"

"No," Harriet shakes her head and looks a little sad. "She left on Friday and it was quite sudden. She told me she'd had enough and he could train his own assistant because she was out of here. It was a sad end to a successful career and I hold Mr Landon responsible. He couldn't even give her the send-off she deserved."

She sighs and then smiles brightly. "Anyway, you don't want to hear about that. Today is all about you and your new exciting role. I'll take you through the general admin and then we can get you settled in. Mr Landon is away from the office today, anyway, so we can settle you in before he bowls in demanding your attention."

As I follow her to personnel, I feel a little deflated. He's not here. Why does that make me feel as if something's missing? I can't help but think back to the last few weeks where I've thought of little else than my impressive new boss. I've imagined all sorts and some it x-rated. I must get a grip because the last thing I need is to develop a super-sized crush on the annoying man who now calls the shots.

It turns out to be an interesting day and I soon find myself relaxing. Alice and Harriet couldn't be kinder and show me to my desk and point out where everything is. Then they leave me to get acquainted with things while they set about organising my security pass and email.

I spend the rest of the day looking through files and familiarising myself with my own office space. Claire, to her credit, has left a list of pointers to help me, which I am extremely grateful for. It makes me laugh when I see a big 'Good luck you're going to need it' written in bold letters at the foot of it but she doesn't need to tell me that. I know already because luck is going to play a big part in making a success out of this job, that's certain.

Now Ronnie has left, I can devote my full attention to my job. If I am worried about him, I push it aside because I can only focus on one thing now and that's my career.

So, when everyone else leaves, I stay. I spend hours poring through the files and making notes. I set up my computer and read through the calendar, familiarising myself with appointments, scheduled meetings and anything imminent. Then I google companies I'm unfamiliar with and the names on the appointment calendar. I make it my mission to find out everything I can, so I'm prepared for anything because I know that Julian Landon will expect it.

Luckily, the cleaning company that I worked for replaced me with someone who doesn't know me and I watch with interest as she does the very job I used to. She keeps her distance because I am working when no one else is and I feel so grateful that I took a chance and went for this position because look at me now.

It must be 8pm before I feel the tiredness taking over and I shut down my computer and head for the lift. As first days go, this one was the best ever and I feel a great sense of job satisfaction as I head for home.

The train home was quiet because of the time I travelled, giving me a much-needed seat and time to think with no distractions. I thought about Ronnie and the mystery surrounding him. I'm trying not to think the worst, but it's impossible not to. Nothing adds up, and yet everything points to the one possible reason – the missing girls. Surely it wasn't him, but what if it was? This is serious and I fully expect a knock on the door any day from the police or the press.

The same subject is on my mind as I make the short walk from the station to my home. The street lamps illuminate my way, and the only companion I have is my overactive imagination.

I even start to imagine I'm being followed and pick up my pace. I don't know why but it feels as if someone is there, watching and waiting, but for what? Could it be Ronnie, is he waiting to check if the coast is clear?

I daren't turn around to look and am just grateful for the passing cars offering some kind of protection if I am suddenly attacked.

My heart is hammering so fast and my throat is dry. I can feel it, someone's there, and it's not an innocent passer-by either.

As I reach my front gate, I stifle a sob because I hear the footsteps closing in on me. They quicken and I fumble for my keys and my hand shakes as I struggle to unlock the door. The door gives way under my shoulder as I shove it hard and almost fall inside, and then just as quickly, I slam it shut and lock and bolt it, gasping for air as I slump to the floor.

I listen but there is nothing, just the sound of my own rough breathing and I almost cry with relief. That was close. Who was it?

Quickly, I haul myself up and race upstairs, reaching the front bedroom and peering from the corner of the window, the curtains obscuring me from the road outside.

Scanning the street, I look for a shadowy figure watching the house, but there is nobody around. Feeling a little foolish, I rip off my coat and boots and sink down onto the bed and put my head in my hands. What's happening to me? I am so on edge and probably imagining all sorts – I must be, surely?

16

At 8am, I head inside my office and feel a great sense of pride. I did this. Against all the odds, I clawed my way to the top of the ladder by thinking outside the box. No more serving the very people I aspire to be. Now I'm one of them and it feels so good.

The door to Mr Landon's office is slightly ajar and I feel nervous as I hesitate outside, wondering if I should go in.

Then I hear a terse, "Well, come in then and stop making the place look untidy."

Quickly, I do as he says and swallow hard as I see the man himself looking at me with interest. As usual, he is looking so good it makes my heart beat just a little faster and makes me lose the power of speech. Then he leans back and says, "Sit."

Without thinking, I do as he says – we will work on his manners when I have my feet under the table a little more.

"I must say you've disappointed me already, Mrs Carter."

My heart sinks. "I'm sorry, sir, please explain."

His eyes dance with the excitement of a bully taunting its victim as he says shortly, "You're late, which means my coffee is too."

"What do you mean, I'm early? I'm not supposed to start until 9?"

"Correction, Mrs Carter, your contracted hours are 9-6 but I expect you here when I arrive which is 7am and you leave when I tell you. You are my personal assistant and I need you to be available at all times."

I know he's being unreasonable and Harriet Masters would definitely have something to say about this, and yet I wonder if he's just testing me. I wouldn't put it past him, but I can't take that chance, so I just nod. "Of course, I won't make the same mistake again."

He nods and then turns to his screen and I'm unsure what to do next. After an awkward silence, he barks, "Still here, Mrs Carter? My coffee, if it's not too much trouble."

Quickly, I scrape back my chair and almost run from the room. I can't believe that man. How rude can one person be? This can't be right. Do people really get away with speaking to others like that? Then it hits me. He just did. I made it easy for him and set myself up for failure because if I give into him even once, it gives him the mandate to carry on doing it.

My legs shake as I take my seat at my desk and wonder what on earth to do? If I do as he says, I don't have the power to refuse next time. If I don't get his damned coffee, he may decide I'm not the assistant for him.

Erring on the side of caution, I head toward the kitchen and decide to suck it up this once. When Harriet arrives, I'll have a word and ask her advice.

However, I'm still fuming when I deliver his coffee and knock loudly on his door. I hear nothing, so just head inside anyway and see him standing at the window with his phone pressed to his ear. He is talking loudly and appears to be arguing with someone, so I set his coffee down and turn to leave.

"Wait."

His terse command stops me in my track and I raise my eyes to see him watching me with an irritable expression.

He cuts his call and says angrily, "Bloody incompetents. Now, fetch me the Davidson file and be snappy about it. You took far too long with the coffee, which doesn't fill me with hope that you're the person I've been looking for."

The tears burn behind my eyes, but I won't give him the satisfaction of seeing how he got to me. So, I just nod and head back outside and search for the file among Claire's impeccable filing system. Thanking God for Claire, I locate the file easily and head straight back into the lion's den.

As I place the file on his desk with no words spoken, he gestures to the seat in front of him and says bluntly, "Sit."

Feeling like a dog obeying its master, I do as he says, eager not to antagonise the complete and utter bastard that holds my future in his hands.

I must sit there for at least ten minutes while he studies the papers before him and then he looks up and I see a gleam of excitement in his eyes. "The information you fed me regarding Slater has stirred up an interesting predicament."

I say nothing but look at him with an eagerness that has pushed aside any hatred I have for the man looking at me so keenly. "This file is one we've been working on for some time. It's a company on its knees with no hope of recovery. The share price has plummeted and the receivers are circling the carcass as we speak. Slater obviously discovered something of significant value regarding this company because they have received a bid from an interested party who has agreed to take the business on for just £1 and pay off the debts in return."

He leans back and grins. "I had a guy I use to dig a little deeper on the back of your information and he discovered the company have hit on a solution for waste management that will solve the world's landfill problems and reduce them by at least 20% in the first year alone, increasing in volume in the next five years. With the correct finances in place, this company could be worth billions and we are writing it off as dead in the water."

I'm not even remotely sure why he's telling me this, but look at him with a shared excitement and he laughs softly. "Well done, Mrs Carter, you just earned your first brownie point. Without your information, I would be wrapping this one up and burying them in the deepest grave possible. However, now…"

He leans forward and taps his pen on the desk. "Now, I have acquired as many shares as possible, driving up the share price and creating a buzz of excitement. As soon as the markets opened, the share price has increased steadily until it reached an all-time high. Now my shares are worth four times what I paid for them and Mr Slater is having to explain to his contact why he will have to pay above the odds to acquire the shares he so badly needs."

I still feel confused and it must show on my face because he says, "What?"

"I'm sorry, sir, but that was weeks ago. I would have thought the shares would have been sold much sooner than this. Why didn't Mr Slater's contact buy them immediately?"

"Because the company was still trading normally. They have been chipping away at it over the weeks, a little comment in the right ear and a few rumours cast. When you overheard their meeting, the share price was normal. Over the last few weeks, they have created the decline and the markets get very panicked at the merest hint of something going wrong. They wanted this company on the brink before they bought it, which is why I am so pleased with your information. It enabled me to buy the shares at a knock down price before they got their manipulating hands on them. If I sell, I make a substantial profit, if I stay, I make an even greater one. So, thanks to you, I am considerably richer than I was before, as are the clients I instructed to buy. So, for that reason alone, I will overlook your earlier indiscretion and as a reward, treat you to lunch."

I just stare at him in total surprise and he raises his eyes. "Problem, Mrs Carter?"

"Um… no, thank you, sir."

"Then you may go."

I say no more and head back to my desk, completely confused. How have I gone from hating him one minute to looking forward to spending time with him the next?

Maybe it was how I felt when he looked at me with such excitement in his eyes as he shared his good fortune. It could have been when he massaged my ego with tales of how my information made such a difference, or could it be because whenever he looks at me with those velvet brown eyes, something stirs deep inside me. Something I thought was lost years ago and something I thought I'd never feel again. Infatuation.

17

I don't report him to Harriet. I don't even harbour any ill feeling towards him. Instead, I look forward to my lunch date with my boss with a mixture of dread and anticipation. The last lunch I shared with anyone was Ronnie on the day he opened up a can of worms that led to the situation we're in now. I wonder what this lunch will be like compared to that one?

So, at precisely 1pm, he heads outside his office with his tailored jacket slung over his shoulder and looking hotter than any man has the right to look during the working day and nods.

"Ready?"

Quickly, I gather my belongings and almost have to run to keep up with him as he strides towards the lift.

He makes no conversation and I wouldn't know what to say if he demanded it. I'm coming to the conclusion that it's better to wait to be asked than to offer any form of dialogue with this complicated man.

We step inside the lift and he punches the button for the ground floor and leans against the mirrored walls of the elevator. "You intrigue me, Mrs Carter, or can I call you Emma?"

I say in surprise, "You're seriously asking me that?"

"What?" He looks puzzled and I laugh softly, probably the first time I have in his company. "You don't strike me as the type who would ask for anything. I'm guessing if you wanted to call me by my first name, you would and not care if it concerned me or not."

"You have a very low opinion of me, Emma." He raises his eyes and I see a hint of mischief in them.

"I do."

Shrugging, he yawns loudly and then says slightly irritably, "To be honest, you're right. I do what I want, when I want, and to whom I want."

Suddenly, the air is sucked out of the metal-lined box we are travelling in and I feel my pulse racing dangerously. He stares at me long and hard and says darkly, "Does that worry you… Emma?"

He whispers my name so softly I almost don't hear it and find myself fixated on the mouth of the man who sets me on edge. I lean back against the walls for support and say nervously, "I don't know."

"What don't you know?"

"How I feel about you."

He looks at me with a cocky smile and it doesn't surprise me. This man knows full well how powerful he is, which is why he gets away with things no ordinary person would. But he's no ordinary man. No man can hold a candle to this one because he broke the mould when he was created. Cocky, sure of himself and so sexy he should be kept locked away for the protection of society. Paired with a hard edge, he's brutal and cold and dangerous through and through and I have never wanted anyone as much as I do him.

We reach the lower floor and he stands straight and without a backward glance strides from the lift as if he owns the world. I actually think he does because the charisma that surrounds him is a powerful force.

As I scurry behind him, I see the women straighten up and their expressions soften, hoping for his gaze to fall onto them. It doesn't. He ignores absolutely anyone who crosses his path, even the suited men who obviously play a major role in the running of this company.

He sees no one and just heads outside without even checking I'm behind him.

A car is waiting – which doesn't surprise me, and the man that holds the door open nods respectfully as Julian climbs inside with no care for chivalry. I head around to the other side and the man follows me and opens the door courteously. Smiling brightly, I say loudly, "Thank you, you're very kind."

He nods and closes the door behind me.

Inside, the luxury of the car envelops me. Black leather on every surface and gleaming chrome. This car is as clean as if it just left the showroom, and it wouldn't surprise me if it had. I can imagine even cars are disposable to Julian Landon, and I feel a shiver of desire as the power of the man sucks me in and ruins me forever.

Yes, Julian Landon will ruin me, and if I'm sure of anything, it's that.

After ten minutes of silence while he checks his phone and demands no conversation, we pull up outside a smart looking restaurant with a black-and-white striped canopy outside. The man on the door is dressed in a fine red livery, and he opens the passenger door with respect and reverence. Julian moves past him without any acknowledgement and feeling embarrassed, I mouth 'Thank you' to the man and get a smile of appreciation in return.

We are met by a suited man who obviously excels at what he does because he says smoothly, "Good afternoon, sir, madam, your usual table is waiting."

As expected, Julian strides through the smartest restaurant I have ever seen as if he owns it and it wouldn't even surprise me if it turned out that he did.

We follow the man to a table by the window and it is obviously the best table they have because it's both private and yet offers the customer the best view of both the room and the street outside. I take in the starched white tablecloth and polished silver cutlery. The crystal glasses sparkle in the sunlight and the flowers in the centre are fresh and seasonal. The candle that burns low in the glass holder mocks me as if it knows I don't belong here and the padded seats that look both delicate and comfortable wait for us to sit and take delight in the poshest lunch I will probably ever have.

Then it strikes me that there are three seats and three place settings. Somebody is joining us; I wonder who it is.

I am soon put out of my misery because almost instantly I hear a well-educated drawl, "Darling, I'm sorry I'm late."

I look up in surprise and do a double take because the woman joining us is stunning. She could be a supermodel and immediately I compare my own conservative suit with her white, silk trouser suit and costly jewellery that sparkles from her neck, her ears, her wrist and her fingers. Her long dark hair is styled beautifully and her make-up looks as if it was done professionally. I think I just stare open-mouthed as she air kisses Julian and looks at me dismissively as she takes her seat.

Julian smiles and I can't help feeling he is enjoying this way too much as he looks at me and says easily, "Meet Cressida, my beautiful wife." Then he turns to her and says softly, "Darling, this is Emma, she's replaced Claire and today is her first day, so be gentle with her."

His wife flicks her superior gaze over me and then dismisses me out of hand, saying slightly irritably, "You could have told me you were bringing your staff."

"Why should I?"

His tone is sharp and as if he couldn't care less, and she sighs irritably. "Because I wanted to spend

time with you alone. We have things to discuss."
She looks at me and says tightly, "In private."

Watching the two of them is interesting to say the least because they act like mere acquaintances instead of husband and wife. I detect no warmth, no genuine feeling, or even a mutual like for one another. This couple are as empty as Ronnie and I and it takes me all of two minutes to work that out.

Julian shrugs and consults his menu and as the waiter hovers nearby, he actually clicks his fingers and I look at him in disbelief as he says in a voice that demands no argument, "We will all have the house special menu with a bottle of Dom Perignon. Three bottles of water and a garden salad."

He snaps the menu closed and the waiter heads off, leaving me speechless. What just happened, don't we even get to choose our own meals?

His wife doesn't appear bothered and just looks irritated by him and snaps.

"Fine, have it your way. Now, remember I'm off to Paris tonight for a couple of days. I'll be taking the helicopter and the pilot."

"I bet you are." I allow my thoughts to entertain me far more than this couple of wax works and smirk as I take a sip of water, giggling inside at the way Julian's eyes flash as he watches me.

"The girls are home this weekend and I have arranged activities that should keep them out of your hair for the duration. Nicola is going to take them out for a few excursions and she arranged for the Glastonbury's children to visit and attend a sleepover."

He looks alarmed and she smiles a little maliciously and says, "I'm sure you'll cope, darling, maybe one of your lady friends can step up and actually be of some use for a change."

I can't believe they don't remember I'm sitting here as I stare at my place setting awkwardly. This is awful and I wish I was having a sandwich at Pret a manger, in fact, McDonald's would do because this is excruciating.

Julian says with an acid tongue. "You should know about entertaining friends, my darling, you're getting in quite the practice. Maybe you would like to introduce me to these so-called friends of yours one day, that would be interesting."

Her eyes flash and she hisses. "I could say the same for you, darling. I had to have the whole house deep cleaned after my last little trip away because of the stench of cheap trashy perfume that lingered on my bedsheets."

Quickly, I stand and say, "Um… if you'll excuse me."

"Sit down."

His voice is like a whip bringing me to my knees and I sit, shaking in my seat as the waiter delivers the champagne. There is silence as he pours the sparkling liquid into the glasses and then hurries away nervously. My hand shakes as I reach for the glass and for the first time Cressida looks at me and says sharply, "Good luck with your new job, you're going to need it. Maybe you can do me a favour and keep my husband happy and away from me because god knows I can't stand to be a minute more than I have to."

She stands quickly and throws her napkin to the table. "Au revoir, darling, and enjoy your lunch. Don't think I don't know you engineered this little threesome just to avoid the conversation we should really be having. See you next Tuesday, *darling*."

She smirks and strides from the restaurant, and I can't help but giggle inside. I think I hold just a little tinge of respect for Cressida because she has done what I'm guessing nobody else would ever dare to, make her husband look like a complete fool in public.

18

"Did my wife amuse you, Emma?"

I am trying not to laugh, but the light must dance in my eyes because I just nod. "A little."

Luckily, the waiter comes with our salad and I look at it in astonishment. If I was expecting a plate of limp lettuce, I was sorely mistaken. It's as if they have raided the gardener's world allotment and provided a representation of every variety of salad item going. My stomach growls as I stare in admiration at the food, and Julian laughs.

"You like it?"

Nodding, I pick up my fork with an eagerness that kicks any manners I have into touch. "It looks – amazing."

He looks pleased and nods.

"You may eat."

I look at him in surprise and he grins. "You will soon learn that I like to call the shots, Emma. Word of advice – let me."

Shrugging, I start forking the food into my mouth quicker than normal because every mouthful tastes so good. I have to remind myself not to groan out loud because I've never eaten a salad as tasty as this one.

I can feel his eyes on me as I power through the plate and after a while says a little tersely, "My wife's a bitch."

I think I stop chewing and just pretend I never heard him. Then he sighs and pushes his plate of food away.

"What do you see when you look at me, Emma?"

I look at him in surprise, unsure what to say. On the one hand, I see someone who interests me way too much given how rude he is and on the other, I see a man who has it all. Deciding to stick with the safer option, I say carefully, "I think you have it all."

Sighing, he pushes his plate away and stares moodily out of the window.

"That's what they all see but they couldn't be further from the truth."

I'm not sure if he realises that I'm still sitting here because he has an expression on his face that shows he is far away somewhere in his mind that only tortured souls go. There is a lost look about him and it's as if he's let his guard down and it's an amazing sight to see. I watch him with shock mixed with pity because this man is different to the one I came here with. He is almost human and my first instinct is to wrap him up and tell him everything will be ok. I'm not sure why I feel the need to, but it's the sheer helplessness of his expression that calls out to me and makes me want to step up and make it all better.

Then he appears to snap out of it and looks at me with a razor-sharp stare.

"Are you happy, Emma?"

His question takes me by surprise and I go with my first instinct, "Of course."

Leaning forward, he stares deep into my eyes and whispers, "Liar."

I feel the heat spreading through me and it's not just because he obviously sees deep inside my soul. It's because he is looking at me with *that* look, the one that says he is more interested in me than any employer has any right to be. The look of a man interested in a woman for his own pleasure and the one that says he knows he can just click his fingers and I'll come running in every way.

Struggling to get a grip, I fix him with a blank stare, even though inside my hormones are raging out of control. "No, I'm not."

He smirks and I see the excitement spark in his eyes as he whispers huskily, "You can't hide from me, Emma. I see the way you look at me. You are like an open book to me. You try to hide it but from the moment you walked into my office uninvited, I saw the interest in your eyes and I watched with amusement the lengths you went to get ahead."

My mouth is dry and my heart thumps as the man before me analyses me so correctly. He carries on. "I had every reason not to give you this job, Emma. You are unqualified, inexperienced and completely the wrong person for the job. You don't fit in and ordinarily would never have got past the first draft of applicants."

An uneasy feeling creeps over me as I sense the final blow about to be delivered and feel anxious, afraid and as if my entire world could crumble at any second as I stand on the precipice waiting for him to push me over the side.

He leans forward and I feel his breath touch my face, caressing it like the coolest, calming breeze. He says in a slightly husky voice, "I saw a lot of me in you and who couldn't be impressed by that."

He smirks and I feel my hand itching to wipe it off his face because he is so sure he has the measure of me. As I think about it, it annoys me to realise he has. He has seen through my charade and found me lacking. Men like that can smell fear, and he knows I'm now in a world I have no business occupying. He knows I'm one of them, the invisible workers who pass by him every day; never seen, heard, or acknowledged in any way. Women like me don't sit in fancy restaurants mixing with the ones that have it all. We serve them, so I look down with shame and feel the tears build as I realise I've made a huge mistake.

His tone softens as he says, "Look at me."

I hold my breath as I raise my eyes to his and he stares at me with a keen, searching look and says firmly, "Never show weakness and always look a person in the eye, even if you have no right to. Always believe you matter and have the upper hand whether you are right or not. Never let anyone see your weakness and face them with a challenge because if you show an ounce of fear, they will go in for the kill. It no longer matters who you were before you entered my world, it's the person you are now that counts. I don't like weakness in my staff and I employed the strong woman in you, not the quivering wreck you are showing me now. Can you be that strong assistant I need, Emma?"

I gasp and know that in this moment I would just about agree to anything he asks me and nod vigorously, "Of course, I can be what you need."

I'm not sure why I even added that last sentence but we both know I mean every word because he leans back in his chair with a wicked glint in his eye and a smug expression on his face as he realises he's got me cornered.

He says sharply, "Then I want you to find out everything possible about my wife and give me something I can use to bring her to her knees. Don't let me down, Emma, because I won't accept failure on this."

"But…" I can't even form words and as the waiter arrives to take our empty salad plates, I just stare at my boss with a stunned expression. As soon as the waiter leaves, I whisper fearfully, "But how? I'm not a private detective, you know."

His eyes flash and his lip curls as he hisses, "You're a devious woman which means you are the best person for the job. I want you to do what you do best and give me something I can use against her. That woman is breaking me and I am not prepared to let that happen. Now, you will quickly learn that I hired you for the qualities I saw in you that didn't include your administrative skills and my wife has just given us the perfect opportunity."

He breaks off as the waiter arrives with the main course and my appetite deserts me and it's not because of the quite frankly mouth-watering plate of boeuf bourguignon that has been set before me. No, it's the knowledge I have to see this through to pay him back for the opportunity.

He starts to eat and as I stare at my plate, he says tersely, "Eat up, we don't have long."

As I chew the delicious mouthful of food, it turns to dust in my mouth. I feel cornered and slightly used and now know why I was invited here. To meet the woman he wants me to destroy – for him.

19

Somehow, I make it through lunch. Somehow, I manage to look normal when inside my world has been turned upside down again. And somehow, I follow my new boss on legs that haven't stopped shaking since I sat down.

Can I do this, I'm not so sure anymore? Do I have to do this, of course I do, if I stand any hope of keeping my job?

We travel back to the office in the same silence that accompanied us here.

Just before we stop outside Crossline, Julian turns to me and says in a low voice. "I want you to get inside that woman's head. Discover what she does with her day. What she likes, dislikes, who her friends are, everything. I want to know her dirtiest little secret and I expect you to repay me for my generosity in giving you this chance."

He leans even closer and his breath whips around my face, as he says darkly, "I reward my employees well if they please me, Emma. It will be worth your while, I can promise you that."

As the door flies open, I look in surprise at the driver standing there, holding it open courteously. Julian barks, "Go and make a start. I have another appointment to keep and will be gone for the rest of the day."

"But…"

"No buts, Emma, never question me. Now go."

As I exit the car, I watch it take off with a mixture of surprise and anger. Where is he going? I know his schedule and it didn't mention another meeting. In fact, he has three scheduled for this afternoon alone. What's he playing at?

The first person I see when I reach the executive floor is Harriet, and the sight of her lovely smile almost brings me to my knees. "Hey, Emma, how's it going?"

I'm not sure what to say and she must see I'm conflicted because she takes hold of my arm and steers me into her office, saying kindly, "Please, take a seat."

I do as she says and watch as she pours me a glass of water and says firmly, "It's ok, you can tell me."

Can I? Can I tell this woman what just happened? I doubt it, in fact, I know I can't, so I just say sadly, "He is very demanding."

She nods. "And rude. Don't forget that particular characteristic trait."

A half smile makes its way out and she nods with approval. "At least you can smile, it took Claire three months not to burst into tears at the very mention of his name, you're doing well."

My hand shakes as I raise the glass to my lips and I say sadly, "Why is he so… difficult?"

"He always has been. Maybe it comes with being super-hot and successful. Nobody tells you 'no' because when it comes to men like that, the answer is always yes."

She turns away and I detect a slight flush to her cheeks and it strikes me that Harriet has obviously fallen victim to him herself and for some reason, a frisson of jealously passes through me.

She turns to face me and sighs. "Its early days. Mr Landon is difficult; we both know that but he's a fair boss. If he likes you, you'll do well. In order to get him to like you, you must play his game by his rules."

"Even if they go against the ones in our contract?"

"I'm afraid so. Listen, what's on paper is nothing compared to what he'll expect from you. I've seen strong men break down after a sharp word from him. They fear him because he is so sharp, he destroys any notion they have at getting one over him and loves nothing more than destroying a man before he's even hung his coat on the hook ready for the day ahead. In fact, the only person I know who truly gets to him is the one woman he can't appear to shake like an unwanted virus that's taken hold of his body."

I nod. "His wife."

She laughs softly, "Yes, Cressida Landon, super-bitch and his match in every way."

I feel curious and say with a hint of unease, "What do you know about her?"

Harriet scoffs, "That she deserves that title. That she plays him and has no interest whatsoever in their marriage. That she can't stand him and would like nothing more than to be rid of him forever."

"Why don't they separate if they hate each other that much?"

"Because of money." Harriet laughs bitterly, and I wonder how she appears to know so much. Sitting on the edge of her desk, she sighs.

"They both value money higher than happiness. Cressida relies on Julian to fund her lavish lifestyle and give her status amongst her peers. Julian will never leave her because he's afraid she'll take most of his fortune. They hate each other, yet need each other to survive. Don't get me wrong, they make all the right noises in public and you won't find a bad press report or magazine article on the apparently happy couple but it's all show. They are systematically destroying each other and one day that dynamite will explode. I just hope we're not in the district when it does because it's likely to take with it everything around it.

She breaks off and appears a little flustered. "I'm sorry, I'm speaking out of turn and forget I said anything. Do you feel a little better now?"

Placing the glass of water on the desk, I smile with a bravery I certainly don't feel.

"Yes, thank you. It was good to talk."

She nods and then groans. "Sorry, Emma, I have an interview to conduct in five minutes. I really should be going."

"Of course, and… thank you."

She smiles softly. "Anytime. You know my door is always open and my ear friendly and willing to hear you out. Don't be a stranger and don't face this on your own. We're here to help you through what could become a very challenging job."

I laugh softly, "You're right there."

As I walk away, I feel even more confused than I did before. How on earth am I going to find something that will make Julian happy? This job is certainly not shaping up how I thought it would.

20

I throw myself into my work. Not the work I thought I'd be doing, the one given to me by my demanding new boss.

I must spend hours looking on the internet for any little snippet of information about Cressida Landon. I make notes in a notebook and try to build up a picture of the woman Julian married twelve years ago.

Her picture stares out at me from every photograph ever taken and published on social media. I see her attending glittering events with her hand placed possessively on her husband's arm. Earlier ones show the infatuation they shared in the earlier days of their relationship. They look at each other as if they can't quite believe their luck, and that's just the sort of look the rest of us now give them. I see their house, their children and their lives, all laid out before me in glorious technicolour. When you move with the rich and powerful, the rest of us lap it up like thirsty dogs. Exotic holidays, fabulous lunches and glittering galas, showcase the couple at their finest.

If I'm jealous, it's an emotion nothing like the one of fascination because this couple mesmerise me. They are like movie stars and I wonder when it all started to go so badly wrong for them. Surely, they had it all, then why waste it?

By the time the light dims outside and the cleaners move in for the night, I have built up quite the picture of the Landon's. They seep into every crack in my brain and leave a bad taste in my mouth. I'm better than this. I shouldn't be doing this – stalking a woman on the instructions of her husband.

Once again, I think of my boss all the way home and wonder how he spent his day. He never called and any messages I called him with went straight through to voicemail.

His appointments left angry when I told them he had been called away on urgent business and could they reschedule?

Is this normal practice for a man at the top of his game? I'm not so sure, given the looks on the faces of the people who left with disappointment written all over their faces.

I don't even consider my safety as I walk from the station to my home, deep in concentration and obsessing over the lives of the people I have stalked all day.

An owl hoots nearby, making me jump out of my skin, and a car sounds its horn as it waits patiently outside a brightly lit house on the street.

The wind blows and chills my tired body and then I feel it. The fear. Without turning around, I know I am being followed. The sound of footsteps behind me matching my own but slightly offbeat, warn me of approaching danger. I can feel another person behind me and up my pace. They do too, and soon I am almost power walking to create some distance between us.

A man walks out from his gate a few yards ahead and his dog barks as he sees me approaching. He looks with disinterest as I stop sharply and say in a quivering voice, "Excuse me but do you know the way to Wimborne street?"

It's a distraction I need to allow the person following me to pass, but nobody does. I listen to the man with avid concentration, but not for what he's saying.

Nobody has passed me.

Maybe they've gone.

I brave a furtive look behind me and see a man crossing the street further down the road. Was that him? Do I know him?

The man finishes telling me something I already know and I thank him politely and carry on walking, grateful the coast is clear behind me.

Was that just a coincidence, or was the man scared off.

It must be a further five minutes before I almost fall through my front door and quickly lock it behind me. I'm safe. I'm home and nobody can touch me here.

Ripping my coat from my body with more haste than speed, I race into the kitchen and reach for the phone. This is something to do with Ronnie, I just know it and I need some answers and fast because where I have tried to forget that my life is unravelling around me as I concentrate on my new job, I need to deal with the issue of my missing husband once and for all.

The phone rings for a while before he says, "Carl Carter."

"Carl, it's Emma."

"Oh, hi." His voice sounds weary and a little detached and I say quickly, "Have you heard from Ronnie?"

There's a brief silence and then he sighs heavily. "Nothing I'm afraid, I'm sorry, have you?"

My heart sinks. "No, not a word. Do you think…?"

I almost can't get the words out but say in a frightened whisper, "Do you think we should call the police and report him missing?"

"No!" His response is quick and definite and takes me back a little. "Why not?"

"Because he wouldn't want that."

"Screw what he wants, he needs to explain himself. This is an impossible situation, Carl. I'm in limbo here and don't know if he's coming back, fled the country, or lying in a ditch somewhere. I need to know; why can't you see that?"

There's a brief silence and then he says with a sigh. "Listen, I'm not telling the whole truth, I did hear from Ronnie by text a couple of days ago."

I sit down. "And?"

"And he wants to be left alone. He told me he was ok and had to get away for a while to sort his head out. He told me you were both going through a tough time and he needed his space. I wasn't to tell you because it was best that way and he would be in touch when he could but not to worry."

"And you didn't think to tell me any of this?"

I'm angry and it shows in my voice. He sighs and says almost apologetically, "I'm sorry, Emma. I know it's bad, but he is my brother and I have to respect his wishes."

"He's my husband, doesn't that count for something amongst all this brotherly love?"

"Of course, but he told me not to say anything. What happened, Emma, what really went down between you?"

I slam the phone down, seething with anger. How could he contact Carl and not me? Why would he tell him to say nothing unless…?

A cold feeling grips me once again as the reality bites. He's guilty of something and whatever it is concerns me. He is trying to keep me out of it for a reason. Is it to protect me?

Shivering, I sit at the kitchen table and run through every conversation, every look and every possible scenario in my mind. What has Ronnie done and why is he so secretive about it?

21

The days turn into weeks and there's still no word from Ronnie. I have the feeling I'm being watched but am guessing it's in my head because I never see anyone. Julian is proving to be a mountain to conquer and many times I sob in the toilet cubicle as I deal with the cutting remarks and derogatory words, he fires like bullets at me every hour of the day. He belittles me and questions my decisions and makes me feel as worthless as a person can ever feel and he does it well. I am a quivering wreck for most of the day and yet in there are those moments that act as antiseptic and take the bitter sting away. The moments where he graces me with a smile and compliments me on a job well done. The moments where his voice softens as he speaks to me and allows me an extra hour for lunch to go shopping and pick up something nice – his treat. He showers me with money after a particularly brutal verbal assault, almost as if the thin worn paper of value will take the sting away.

Julian Landon is the most complicated man I have ever met, and I have fallen head over heels in love with him.

They say treat them mean to keen them keen and I can vouch for that. The harder he is on me, the harder I try, just desperate for a kind word or a soft look. When I mess up, his tone is cutting and leaves me in a heap on the toilet floor as I struggle to cope with his disappointment in me.

I know this isn't healthy but I come back for more like a drug addict after a high. The lows are soul wrenching and the highs pure ecstasy. Julian Landon is ruining my life and I'm helping him do it.

Today I return to Barrington's. Julian is away on business and I have decided to take an early lunch. I need to surround myself in normality to remind me of when life was simpler. When I walk through the familiar doors, the first person I see is the owner, Calvin Hunter, who looks at me in surprise. "Emma, you look…"

He breaks off because even I know I look amazing. The money I'm now earning has enabled me to have my hair styled professionally. I have spent painstaking hours recreating my make-up from You Tube videos, and the clothes I now wear are purchased from the costlier shops in town that used to be far above my budget. My shoes are Italian leather and my handbag matches them. I am no longer the grey woman with her eyes lowered who still sees everything. I no longer listen out for any snippet of information about the privileged around me because I am now one of them. I still have no friends because people are wary of me. They think I will tell Julian everything they say, and they are right to be cautious. After all, look what happened to Miles Sinclair.

Almost as soon as I told Julian about his designs on Alice and the executive floor, Julian made it his mission to discredit him in every way possible. The poor guy never caught a break and subsequently was driven mad with anger. He was bypassed for promotion and demoted to a junior with no reason given. Julian made sure he was watched like a hawk and it got so bad he left one day and never returned. It still unnerves me to think how many lives have been ruined through just one slip of my tongue. Then again, it sickens me that the power I feel excites me and makes me hungry for more. I am becoming Julian Landon's bitch in every way but the one I crave, and yet he doesn't look at me in that way. If he did, I would be the happiest woman alive, but even I know I'm way below his standards.

"What brings you here, darlin'?"

Calvin looks at me with interest and I shrug. "I couldn't keep away from the coffee, after all, it is the best in London."

As intended my comment pleases him and he reaches for a mug and says warmly, "Then allow me; on the house, of course."

"Is Leah around?" I feel a little disappointed that she's not working and he shakes his head. "Off with flu. I'm run off my feet because Hailey's not due in for half an hour." He looks at me hopefully and I shake my head. "Not happening, Calvin. I'm a customer now and that's how it's going to stay."

Nodding, he sets about making my drink and says with interest, "So, what are you doing now?"

"Admin mainly, at Crossline."

"Man, that's impressive. Well, good for you, it's not often I lose a valued staff member to that organisation."

I smile and take my drink and head towards the window. As Julian's away, I intend on taking a little time out and have a relaxing lunch for once. I don't normally even take one and just grab a sandwich at my desk most days.

I settle down to watch the passing crowds and think about how my life has changed in just a few months. I never imagined I would be living alone and working for a man as powerful as Julian Landon. As I contemplate the well-heeled people passing the window, I see many familiar faces. Employees of Crossline, all desperate to succeed and clawing their way to the top with ruthless tenacity, until somebody pulls them out of the way and watches them fall as they take their place.

Now I am one of them and need to step up my game because Julian's patience is wearing thin regarding his wife, but there's nothing more I can do.

At first, I don't even register it's her, until the glint of the sun off her necklace draws my attention. As I take in the gleaming dark hair, immaculate clothes and supermodel looks, my heart beats a little faster as I see Cressida Landon standing across the road talking into her phone.

She turns and faces the other direction, and it's as if she's waiting for someone. Quickly, I leave my coffee and head outside, not even returning Calvin's cheery goodbye.

Keeping my head down, I head towards her, making sure to blend in with the crowds littering the pavement as they rush from one place to another, conscious of time.

I hide behind a nearby pillar and pretend to be texting someone and strain to listen as she speaks angrily. "Honestly, Oscar, I'm freezing my tits off out here. How much longer? Julian could come out at any minute."

She is obviously unhappy and stamps her feet on the rain-soaked ground. "Hurry up, because if he sees us together, he will know everything. Mind you, I'm coming dangerously close to telling him myself because you are not shaping up at all."

I watch with interest as a large, black Range Rover screeches to a stop and she rolls her eyes. "Finally! Well, open the door you idiot, do I have to do everything?"

I think I hold my breath as the driver jumps out and reaches for the door, and she steps inside without even a look or a smile. Luckily for me, I decided to photograph this encounter because I get a good shot of the number plate and make and model as it screeches away. I wonder who was in that car and why would they take such a chance in broad daylight in full view of the office her husband works at?

Quickly, I head back inside and straight to security. Julian replaced the previous guard with one from a reputable agency after learning that Mr Slater had installed his own particular spy and Jack the current one is extremely personable and I like him a lot. There is nothing shady about Jack and I say innocently, "Jack, darling, I don't suppose you know who this car belongs to, do you? It almost ran over a cyclist out there."

He looks angry, which I knew would be the case because Jack is a keen cyclist himself and cycles all around London, so he frowns and looks at the picture on my phone.
Quickly he taps the registration into his computer and whistles. "Man - typical."

"What?"

"Mr Slater. It would be, wouldn't it?"

"What do you mean?"

"One of the fucking untouchables, isn't he? He gets away with everything the rest of us would be prosecuted for. I bet he didn't even care that he almost killed someone."

"I don't think he was driving, Jack, you can't heap the blame on him."

He shakes his head. "Maybe not, but I'm guessing he instructed his driver to move off that quickly. I can't stand the man, never have liked him, never will."

"Why not?" I'm curious as to why Jack would dislike Mr Slater so obviously and he sneers. "It's best you don't know. Your delicate ears shouldn't hear stuff like that."

"Like what?" I can feel my eyes are bright and the curiosity is burning me up inside and Jack laughs and leans forward, whispering, "Women visit that man after hours. It's common knowledge with the security staff. Sometimes as late as midnight and sometimes during the working day. He has many visitors that aren't the usual type, if you know what I mean"

He laughs at my expression and whispers, "Escorts, young girls, prostitutes or some poor smuck who actually believes his lies. He's had them all and we have watched."

"Watched?"

He grins. "Yes, the idiot obviously forgot we film 24/7. He's not completely stupid though and conducts his business inside his executive bathroom, but we know. We see the girls come out looking worse the wear for his attentions and we see the disgust on their faces as they grab their stuff and go. Word is, he's a kinky sod, which just about goes with the territory."

"What do you mean?" My voice sounds weak even to my own ears as he says roughly, "They're all at it. All the big wigs upstairs always want to push the boundaries just a little bit further. They have all the money they can spend and it's still not enough. They use that money to buy excitement and danger and get off on the ones that are riskier and a little extreme."

He obviously remembers his place and stands back, saying loudly, "Anyway, you didn't hear that from me." Tapping his nose, he says with a wink. "Discretion is a key part of any security's man's job and if it ain't illegal, it's allowed."

I nod and walk away with the conversation buzzing in my ears. I must get my hands on that footage because I'm guessing there are a lot of answers on that recoding that I badly need right now.

22

A few days later Julian calls me into his office and by the look in his eyes it's not to give me a pay rise.

"Sit."

As usual, I do as I say, having learned early on this is the smallest battle in a long painful war that is best left.

I can tell he's irritated and dig my nails into the palm of my hand as I wait for the telling off I usually get.

"Is there any progress on that project I set you?"

"A little."

He exhales sharply. "I don't *want* a little, I don't *expect* a little, I *demand* a lot."

Counting to ten in my mind, I wait for him to speak rather than answer him.

He leans back in his chair and fixes his entire attention on me, and it's a lot to deal with. When he does this, the walls close in on me and I struggle to breathe. It's as if he sees inside my soul and takes the information he needs and discovers it's not useful to him. Then he looks at me with disgust, leaving me eager to replace that look with one of admiration. How have I fallen so far as to crave any form of praise from a tyrant?

He says angrily, "Well?"

My voice sounds weak as I stutter, "Your wife met with Mr Slater on Tuesday at 12pm."

I see a spark of interest in his eyes and he leans forward. "And?"

Reaching for my phone, I show him the photograph and say quickly, "I discovered this car was Mr Slaters when I questioned the security guard on duty. He let slip that Mr Slater likes to entertain women in his office, both late at night and through the day."

Julian snorts. "Dirty old sod, I wonder what his wife Miriam would think of that?"

I smile slightly. "Not a lot I'm guessing."

Tapping his fingers on the desk, he says thoughtfully. "And Cressida went off with him in this car, I wonder why?"

"I think they're working together."

His eyes fall on me sharply and I say quickly, "I heard her say she couldn't risk you seeing her waiting for him. That if you did, you would know what they were up to immediately. She also told him he wasn't shaping up and she was of half a mind to tell you herself."

"Did she now?"

Julian looks animated and I can only wonder what is going through his mind and then he looks at his Rolex and smiles thinly. "Call my driver, we're going on a road trip."

"What?"

My voice is shaky and he says briskly, "Don't ask me questions, just deal with it. Call my driver and grab your coat. Do you understand that simple request, or do I need to put it in a power point presentation?"

"But your appointment?"

He shrugs. "Email them from the car and cancel. We have important work to do."

I jump up and leave him to sort himself out and quickly shut my computer down and grab my iPad. Then, by the time I've grabbed my coat and handbag, he is striding from the office as I have become accustomed to.

I follow him like an Arab's wife, ten paces behind as he sweeps into the elevator and presses the button for the ground floor with an irritation that accompanies him everywhere.

I daren't speak as I can tell he is deep in thought and as I follow him out to the street, I wonder where we are going in such a hurry.

His driver is waiting and as usual, he arranges himself in his seat without caring how I join him. He barks at the driver, "Home."

Then he raises the glass partition that separates us and I sit shaking as he says in his sexy deep voice. "This is our chance, Emma. By the sounds of it, Cressida is up to no good with Slater and we can use this time to our advantage."

"But what if she's home, with Mr Slater?"

Julian laughs. "Then all the better. I hope they are because it would make this easier but knowing Cressida, they are hidden away somewhere no one will ever find them while they plot against me."

"What makes you think they're plotting against you?"

He turns to face me and his eyes flash dangerously. "Don't be obtuse, Emma. Everyone is against me. When you hold the position I do, there's only way and it's down. Don't you think I know the next one is crawling up the ladder to topple me. They all want this - the power, the fame of being top man, and they don't care how they get it either. Slater's been after my job for years and thinks he can get it through my wife."

He laughs softly. "He's welcome to try. I mean, he wouldn't be the first and definitely won't be the last. No, I intend on protecting myself the only way I know how."

I daren't ask but somehow my voice has other ideas because it says shakily, "How?"

He laughs and faces me with a look that shows the power of the man as he hisses, "I'll destroy them both as only I can."

I feel weak and settle back against the upholstered leather, and Julian smiles in a sinister way. "Do you like power, Emma?"

My breath hitches. "Yes." My voice sounds small and weak, nothing like it should when talking about power. He inches closer and I feel his leg hard against mine as he whispers, "Does it turn you on?"

Oh, if only he knew. My breath is ragged as I gasp, "Yes."

I watch as his hand reaches down and lingers over my knee. I watch with my breath hitched as it hovers over the hem of my skirt and I lick my lips, willing it to make contact with my skin.

His face is closer now and he whispers in my ear, "Do you want me, Emma?"

I sense the victory already in his eyes rather than see it for myself as I say softly, "Yes."

He sits back against the chair and says coolly, "Yes, they all do. It can become a little tiresome after a while. You see, nobody likes a sure thing, Emma. They like a challenge and someone who resists their charms. Someone who fights to get away and someone who doesn't fall for their bullshit. You're just like the rest of them - easy. You disappoint me."

He turns to his phone, leaving me broken inside. How can he be so cruel? At this moment I hate Julian Landon with a passion and it must be steaming off me in waves because he laughs softly, "Harness your anger and your passion, we will need it later."

Taking deep breaths, I stare at the blurred landscape through the window of the speeding car and decide in that moment that I really, really hate and detest Julian Landon.

23

Wow. I thought it would be impressive, but this place – Julian's home, is absolutely stunning. On the outskirts of London lies a sweeping estate that has his name on it. We pass through an impressive set of electric gates and along a driveway that is flanked by ornamental trees. I am pretty sure they even clean the stones that make a pleasing crunch as we drive over them because there is not even a blade of grass out of place in this immaculate palace.

As I stare at perfection, he says with amusement. "Do you like it?"

My earlier anger towards him evaporates as I say with excitement, "Of course, who wouldn't?"

Like a kid in the sweetshop, I devour the view before me, taking everything in and refrain from clapping my hands like an excited child.

The car appears to take forever to stop outside an impressive portico and the large wooden door that stands proudly waiting wouldn't look out of place on a castle.

As soon as the car stops, Julian is out and I quickly follow, almost running to see inside a place I never thought I'd visit.

The door is not even locked and when we head inside, I see why because a woman heads over to greet us dressed in a black skirt and white blouse.

"Good morning, Mr Landon, I wasn't expecting you."

He says tersely, "Coffee, Nicola, and we'll have it in my study."

Feeling her pain, I follow him across a beautiful marble tiled hallway, that is bigger than my entire house and I don't even have time to enjoy the opulent surroundings before I find myself in his study. I almost can't breathe. He is *everywhere*.

The scent of his aftershave lingers in the air, mixed with wood smoke and the evidence of a cigar or two. The polished wood gleams and the window looks out on an ornamental garden that could be opened to the public, it's that amazing.

His huge desk dominates the room and set around it is comfortable seating and a massive television that is set into the word panelling. A shelf containing decanters filled with wicked looking liquid sparkle for attention and I am blown away.

Pointing to an upright chair in the corner of the room, he barks, "Sit!"

Once again, I do as he says, hating myself just a little more because I don't stand up for myself as my self-worth and pride slip dangerously away.

He flicks on his computer and appears to be searching for something as Nicola heads into the room, balancing a tray precariously. I jump up to help and he says firmly, "I said, sit."

Raising her eyes, she sets the tray down on a small table near an impressive fireplace and says courteously, "Would you like me to serve you?"

"No, my assistant will do the honours, you may go."

He says it without even looking at her, and she throws me a pitying glance as she heads outside the room. Unsure what to do next, I say a little on edge, "Shall I be mother?"

I say it brightly in the vain hope it may inject a little humour into a tense situation and am rewarded by a sharp look and a terse, "Just pour the god-damned coffee and keep your smart remarks for your spare time."

Once again, his attention switches to the screen and feeling like a battered punching bag, I do as he says – as usual.

I must sit for thirty minutes in silence as I sip my coffee and take in the glorious view. I'm not even talking about the one through the large picture window, but the man who sits before it. Yes, Julian Landon could make me watch him all day because he is that perfect.

Finally, he shouts triumphantly, "Ok, I'm in and now you need to step up and do some work for a change."

Feeling the bitterness return, I look at him with pure hatred flashing from my eyes as he laughs softly. "Cressida's password-protected file. It's taken me thirty bloody minutes to crack the code, but it's done and I'll leave you to discover what you can. Don't change anything, just photograph the evidence. I'll be back later."

"What, you're leaving me here, what if...?"

"She comes back, so what? Say you're under orders away from the office. She won't ask, though."

"Why not?"

"Because it's not unusual. Nearly all of my assistants come here and work at some time or another. Nothing new here."

I feel a little miffed that this is nothing unusual and he laughs softly. "You are nothing special, Emma. Deal with it."

As he heads outside, he says over his shoulder. "I'll be about two hours and then I'll take you to dinner. Make sure you earn it."

The door slams, leaving me feeling bruised, battered and emotional. How can I hate him so much I can actually taste it like a rancid poison inflicting a long, slow, painful death on me and love him just as hard? I hate myself more than him at this moment in time, and yet I push any feelings I have aside and get on with the job in hand.

Soon I discover that Cressida Landon likes to spend money. Details of her credit card make interesting reading, and I can only imagine what it must feel like to be able to afford absolutely anything you want, even from the most expensive shops.

Along with clothing, jewellery and accessories are details of restaurant reservations and mini breaks. Her airline bill is eye watering and I can't even pronounce some of the places she has gone to.

She spends just as much money on her home and her children and as I see fees for private schools and extra-curricular activities, I feel a knot of jealously forming inside me. How can two disgusting, horrible people have so much beauty surrounding them? It's not fair that life is so generous to the wickedest people of society, when the good have so little. They have no manners and no idea of how to talk to any unfortunate person who crosses their path. If it wasn't for their money, I doubt they would be surrounded by so many people and I couldn't hate them anymore than I do as I sit in their magnificent home and wish it were mine.

Around an hour after Julian left, Nicola pokes her head around the door and says kindly, "I brought you something to eat."

My stomach growls, reminding it that I skipped lunch and I stare at her gratefully. "You are so kind, thank you."

She beams happily, probably because she never gets thanks, and heads into the room with a silver platter of dainty little sandwiches and delicious looking pastries. "I'll bring the tea in just a second, is there anything else I can get for you?"

"A new job." I groan out loud as the screen swims before my eyes and she laughs.

"Well, if you find one, remember me."

"I will, Nicola, don't you worry about that."

She turns to leave and I say quickly, "How long have you worked here?"

She looks surprised. "Four years I think."

"Wow, you deserve a medal. Have they always been this, well, uptight, really?"

Nicola laughs. "Sadly, yes, although they were a lot more loving towards each other when I first arrived. Now though, well, let's just say they're better when they live here at different times."

"It must be hell."

"It is." She sighs and looks so upset I feel bad for raising the subject.

"It's those poor little girls I feel sorry for."

I look at her with interest and her gaze falls to the polished silver frame on Julian's desk, where two perfect Angels smile for the camera.

"Imogen and Amelia. Two beautiful darlings who don't deserve the parents fate inflicted on them."

"They are both so pretty."

"Is it any wonder with the parents they've got? Luckily, they haven't inherited their manners because two sweeter girls you would struggle to meet."

I look at her with interest and almost don't ask, but she says bitterly, "You're wondering why I stay."

I just nod and she sighs and pulls up a chair. "For them, really. The two girls. Their parents are always happier being anywhere but with them, so I endure this harsh environment to care for them. To be honest, I prefer it when they're not here because they take the dark clouds with them wherever they go."

"What do you mean, dark clouds?"

"You know what I mean, dear. They surround the pair of them, bringing anxiety and depression into a room. They may be intelligent people, but they're clueless about real life. Mr Landon can switch between being sweet and kind one minute to Satan with a click of his fingers. Mrs Landon is always mean and never has a nice word to say to anyone. If I'm honest, I wish they would just split up and be done with it. I'm sure they'll end up killing each other, which would be the best outcome all round if you ask me."

She grins as I stare at her in shock and moves towards the door. "Anyway, I should get to work. Just call if you need anything, the numbers on the phone."

Looking down, I see the phone has several extensions and judging by the size of the house, I'm not surprised. I see housekeeping, kitchen, gardener and handyman listed to name but a few.

Struggling to come to terms with how the other half live, I turn my attention back to the computer and spend the next hour gathering even more information, although none of it appears to be that damning if you ask me.

However, as I finish up, I notice an icon on the desktop that looks a little different to the others. It looks out of place because it's a picture of a child's drawing and entitled *Amelia's memories*. Thinking that maybe Cressida isn't such a bad mother after all, I click on it hopeful of finding that she is a little human, but it's not what I expect. It appears to be a series of spreadsheets detailing deposits made into an account entitled, 'Retirement fund.'

My eyes water at the size of the numbers entered neatly in their little rows, and I gasp at the frequency they are deposited. Unless I'm mistaken, Cressida Landon is fleecing her husband dry behind his back. Either that, or she has a side line that pays more than the national debt.

Quickly, I photograph the evidence and hearing footsteps outside on the marble floor, quickly exit the programme and click on the internet just as Julian heads into the room.

He looks weary and preoccupied, and I wonder where he's been for the past two hours.

Without any of the usual niceties, he snaps, "We're leaving."

I stand quickly and make way for him as he shuts the computer down and then spins on his heels and marches from the room.

However, he doesn't head to the front door and instead marches towards a door to the rear of the impressive hallway. It leads to a state-of-the-art kitchen and my eyes bulge as I see the result of every wet dream a woman has ever had. Designer doesn't cut it because this kitchen is one of a kind. It's so big I could lose myself in it and my mouth waters at the gleaming granite surfaces and handmade painted units. A huge Aga dominates the space and along with every modern gadget going, the place sparkles as if it's never been used. A bank of floor to ceiling cupboards must be home to the white goods a kitchen of this size must require, but they are hidden behind outstanding carpentry and I wish I had longer to absorb this little piece of heaven.

Julian strides through a side door, through a massive utility and boot room, outside onto the perfect lawn a green keeper would die to maintain. My eye is drawn to a sound just beyond the perfect hedging, and I gasp as I see a helicopter waiting patiently for our approach. Stopping abruptly, I say in amazement. "You're kidding me."

"Do I look like I am?" Julian sounds irritable and doesn't break his stride as he marches towards the beast waiting for us.

Impatiently, he pushes me towards the steps and almost manhandles me into the back of the gleaming helicopter.

As he jumps in beside me, he yells, "Paris."

Then he says firmly, "Buckle up and shut up."

Wishing with all my heart I could tell him where to shove his helicopter, I do as he says because now is not the time to challenge him. However, as I fight back the tears, I've come to the conclusion that my days are numbered working for this man. As soon as I can, I am drafting my resignation letter and sticking it up his ass.

24

I am in complete awe of Paris. The fact it's still light enables me to see clearly the magnificent city below and I gasp with delight at the landmarks that I'm used to seeing in films and on the television. Julian hasn't said two words since we left and is obviously brooding about something.

He stares at his phone and occasionally I steal a glance and my eyes water as I see him staring at pictures of his beautiful daughters. Seeing this side of him melts my earlier anger because it's obvious he loves them. Just the way his gaze lingers on their dear little faces as he scrolls through his camera roll. There are none of his wife from what I can see and I wonder about him. Is he really such a big bad wolf all the time? I hope not for those girl's sake.

We soon land on top of a skyscraper and as the rotor blades slow down, he yells, "Come on."

Wrenching open the door, he jumps out, pulling me with him, and I duck and hold my hair in place as we run for cover.

I feel as if I'm in a film and can't believe how my life has changed, but as soon as we're inside, he snaps. "Listen and take notes. That's all you're here for."

Feeling a little curious, I follow him down the stairs until we reach a lift. We then travel to the fourteenth floor and as we exit, I take in the sumptuous surroundings of what appears to be an affluent company. All around me is French chic at its finest and not for the first time, I feel a little lacking in my own choice of clothing.

The women here are cool and beautiful, wearing tailored suits paired with silk blouses. Their hair is styled to perfection as is their make-up and I feel like something that blew in off the pavement outside.

I hate that Julian looks as if he's just stepped out of men's Vogue and speaks to the woman who met us in fluent French.

We head towards what appears to be a huge boardroom and I gasp as I see the Eiffel Tower standing proudly outside.

Julian greets a man who stands to shake his hand, and I look with interest at the several men sitting around the table. Their assistants appear to sit slightly behind their boss and sighing, I do the same behind mine.

Then begins the most tedious meeting of my life as they discuss share options and wealth management. I take notes and try to look interested, but I am dying inside.

After a while, I decide to cheat a little and quickly flick record on my phone. I can't keep up with taking the notes and would much rather stare at the surrounding people instead. As always, my gaze falls to Julian and my heart flutters. He is easily the most attractive man in the room, and despite how much I hate him, I would pay good money for just one night with him. It amuses me to think of him as a sort of male prostitute for my enjoyment, and just for a moment, I indulge the fantasy a little. As I stare around the circle of people, I shiver inside. These people are so different to the usual types I mix with. I would not be surprised if the air they breathe is laced with power because each one of them has that look about them that sets them above the rest of us.

One man in particular catches my attention, and I suppose it's because he is on the edge of the group. It's his expression that gives him away because the hatred he is directing at Julian is almost palpable. However, his face switches to a blank mask when he is looking and I wonder who he is. There's an animosity between them that's obvious to me, anyway. I listen carefully when he speaks and it's usually to contradict something Julian says, or to offer a differing opinion on the way they should all move forward. The other attendees don't appear to notice anything out of the ordinary and I soon start fidgeting as I fully expect the guy to brandish a gun and shoot Julian dead on the spot.

I distract my attention from him by studying the other assistants in the room and am pleased to see at least two of them are men. In fact, there are a couple of women joining in the meeting, which makes me happy. However, the focus in the room is on Julian and the man who stood to greet us. They are discussing ways of making even more money through some sort of hedge fund, and if I could stick pins in my eyes to relieve the boredom, I would.

It must be two hours later that the men stand and the rest follow. Julian shakes their hands and then, without even the courtesy of an acknowledgement, strides from the room, leaving me scurrying after him, as has become the norm it seems.

He heads back the way we came and as soon as we appear on the roof, the helicopter pilot gives Julian the thumbs up and starts the blades, leaving us to scramble inside the helicopter and fasten our seatbelts.

By now I am so hungry I could eat my notebook and hope the restaurant isn't far. However, Julian appears to have had a change of heart and growls, "Take us back to the office."

I look at him in surprise, because by now it's 6pm and the thought of working late is not a happy one.

I know better than to ask what's going on and just wait while he looks through his own leather-bound notebook at the various notes he made during the meeting. After checking his phone, he says, "I trust you took notes."

Feeling a little guilty, I nod. Then his hand reaches out and he says abruptly, "I want to see them."

Handing over my notebook like a student found cheating, he flicks through the pages and then throws it back at me. "And the rest, or did you just get bored and study your nails?"

"Of course not."

He raises his eyes and I shrug. "I recorded it and will transcribe it tomorrow."

Leaning back, he looks annoyed. "Why?"

"Because I couldn't keep up and preferred to watch the people around you. You can tell a lot more from doing that than any old note taking."

I think I've gone too far because Julian looks astonished, and then he laughs softly. "Good call, Emma. You continue to surprise me."

Basking in the increasingly rare praise, I feel a little smug and he says, "So, what did you discover when you studied my colleagues?"

"That Mr Bivier hates and detests you with a passion."

He nods. "I know."

I can't help but laugh. "I suppose it was a bit obvious. I'm guessing he's after your job, or the contract, one of them at least."

Julian nods. "Yes, another one who joined the line. He's an idiot, though. He's always let his anger get the better of him, and in most situations, it's best kept under wraps. You may have noticed he sat a short distance away and that's because he wasn't considered important enough."

Wow, poor Mr Bivier, he must have hated that.

Julian looks at me with interest. "What did you discover at the house?"

Suddenly, I feel excited as I whip out my phone and scroll to the spreadsheet photos. "It appears that

Cressida is building herself quite the retirement fund."

I hand him the phone and he looks at the screen with astonishment. "This was on her computer?"

I nod. "Filed under *Amelia's memories*. Maybe she thought it would draw less attention to it and would be overlooked."

Julian nods. "She's right there. Maybe I've underestimated her, she's almost got more money than me."

"Are you sure it's not your money?"

He laughs, and for the first time since I met him, I see him look at me with a new expression in his eyes – respect.

It knocks me for six as I bask in the unfamiliar. He is impressed and it feels so good.

The helicopter starts its descent and Julian offers me a rare smile that totally transforms him. He was always good-looking but now he is beautiful. The smile softens his features and makes him look almost human, and it's as if the cares and worries melt away and he is free of trouble for the first time since I met him.

As the helicopter lands, he reaches out and grasps my hand, squeezing it softly. Then he says something I never thought I'd hear from his lips. "Well done, Emma. Good work, you have made me very happy."

He releases my hand and exits the helicopter, leaving me stunned behind him. That was – unexpected, and suddenly my resignation letter fades into the past where it belongs. Now I've got the measure of the man and I like what I see and maybe, just maybe, this could work.

25

Julian doesn't buy me dinner as promised, but it doesn't matter. Nicola called and told him there was a drama at the girl's school and Mrs Landon was incommunicado. It made my heart lift to see the concern in Julian's eyes as he hurried off to deal with the problem, leaving me to head home as usual, alone, tired and hungry.

However, tonight I walk on a cloud as I replay the moment when I earned his approval. I suppose I did well today, even by my own standards because I saw how much my information would benefit him.

I wonder about his wife and the game she is playing, but that doesn't concern me. What does, is that I make a go of this and prove to everyone that someone with nothing can achieve their dreams? Because now my dreams have changed and I want more than I ever thought I deserved. I want what they have and I don't care how I get it. Money is a powerful aphrodisiac and the ruin of men. It sucks you in and promises the world and people will do anything to grasp it for themselves. I am no exception and can't see past my own desire to live the life I have been privy to today.

Thinking of my life before Julian, makes me realise just how right I was to do everything I could to get ahead. It's opened my eyes and I like what I see and has made me even more determined to forget where I've come from and concentrate on where I'm going instead.

I forget any anxiety I may have as I walk from the station to my house. I forget my earlier fears as I rack my brains to think about how I can make more money and I completely forget about my husband who is irrelevant to me now until I am aware of another person close behind me and my heart races with fear. Quickly, I increase my pace and move quicker, almost a run. My heart starts pounding as I gasp for air to aid my progress but it's all in vain because a hand reaches out and grabs my arm and a voice says loudly, "Mrs Carter, please stop."

I turn in surprise because the voice that spoke was a woman's voice and as I spin around, I find myself facing a familiar face. It takes just a few seconds for the face to fit and I pull back as I realise it's the woman from the pub. I think her name was Caroline; wasn't she the wife of one of Ronnie's card playing friends?

She looks at me with fear in her eyes and says breathlessly, "Please, hear me out but we may be being watched and don't have long."

I stare at her in horror as she propels me down a dark alley towards the recreation ground and looks about her furtively. I hiss, "What's going on, what do you want with me?"

She places her finger to her lips and I am astonished when her eyes fill with tears and she whispers, "Have you seen Ronnie?"

I shake my head and her face crumbles and I can see she is destroyed. My curiosity is now at maximum levels and I say softly, "I don't live far, come back and we'll talk."

She nods and says urgently, "I'll follow, leave the door ajar, I need to check the coast is clear first."

I nod but feel extremely worried as I make my way home, leaving her to follow closely behind.

It doesn't take long and I soon reach my home and once again, rush inside looking around me in fear for what may be waiting. However, as usual, the house is cold and empty, reminding me that the life left here months ago and is now just a place to lay my weary head at night and recharge for the next challenging day.

"Quickly, I crack open a bottle of wine and take a large gulp. I'm not normally a drinker, but fear I'll need the courage tonight because something in her expression told me I am not going to like what I hear.

The door creaks open and I jump a little. Then I relax as I see Caroline venturing inside, looking so worried it sets me on edge.

She quickly bolts the door behind her and then promptly bursts into tears.

I stare at her in shock as she crumbles before me. Unsure as to what on earth is happening, I move towards her and say gently, "Come on, let's get you inside and you can tell me what's bothering you."

She nods and follows me to the kitchen and I guide her to the chair by the counter and say as reassuringly as I can, given the weird situation, "I'll make you a cup of tea."

As she sits sniffing into a tissue, it strikes me just how weird my life became since Ronnie left. Seeing Caroline in our kitchen is a little strange and I prepare myself for what I think she's about to tell me. The strangest thing of all is that I don't care. If Ronnie's been having an affair with this woman, it almost makes me happy because if I've learned anything these past few weeks, it's that I don't want him anymore.

As I hand her the tea, she takes it gratefully and looks at me with tortured eyes. Sitting opposite, I steel myself for what's coming and after a few moments, she says, "You're in danger."

Well, I didn't expect that and it must show on my face because she nods emphatically. "I know it sounds far-fetched but please believe me, it's true."

"But why? How on earth can I be in danger – from Ronnie?"

My voice quivers as I say his name because suddenly, I see him that day in the bedroom when he lost his temper. I remember the way his fists balled when he spoke to Caroline at the pub, and I recall the desperation in his eyes as he sat silently staring at the television screen. Then I think about the conversation I overheard in the coffee shop as the two girls discussed the missing girls and hinted at the possibility it could be a cab driver. My heart freezes as I pray to God she isn't going to tell me that.

Once again, her face crumbles and she sobs, "I'll start at the beginning but I must apologise in advance for what I'm about to tell you."

She looks at me keenly, but I give nothing away and she sighs. "Ronnie used to come to the poker games my husband ran every Friday night. He was good at it and often won, which used to irritate my husband." A small smile graces her lips and her eyes get that wistful look as she remembers a happier time. "I used to love watching them. I kept them fed and watered, but I could never take my eyes off Ronnie."

She blushes a little and my heart hardens. "He was always so calm and controlled, nothing like Stuart, my husband. He was, and still is, a difficult man to please and his rages were things to avoid at all costs. I suppose things changed for Ronnie and me when I saw him in town one day. He was always so kind and polite and I was carrying some heavy bags which he offered to help me with. He asked if I fancied a coffee and we spent a lovely hour just chatting and laughing, something I didn't do a lot of with Stuart. The next time I saw him at the card game, he looked at me a little differently. We shared a few looks that night and the next day when Stuart was at work, he showed up at my door."

Now I feel *my* fists balling and feel the rage boiling beneath the surface – how could he?

"We never meant for anything to happen, but it was as if we were two sides to the same coin. We arranged to meet for lunch and that turned into a more regular thing."

She looks down and I steel myself for the inevitable as she says in a whisper, "I'm ashamed to say we started an affair. I suppose it was easy because we could meet in the day when you were at work and so was Stuart." She looks at me with a little hint of steel in her eyes and says firmly, "I'm sorry, Emma, but I don't regret a minute of the time I spent with Ronnie."

I'm not sure what to say. Should I start shouting and calling her every name under the sun? Should I manhandle her to the door instead of watching her sip the tea that I prepared for her in the delicate bone china mug? I actually feel exhausted as I slump in my seat and put my head in my hands and the tears burn like acid rain behind my eyes. Ronnie cheated on me and I never suspected it for one minute.

She says almost nervously, "We knew it was wrong but couldn't stop something we both wanted more than anything. Then things went wrong and it all unravelled."

The fear returns to her voice and I look up sharply. She looks around nervously and says in a small voice, "We made plans to run away. I wanted to escape an abusive marriage and Ronnie wanted to save me. We needed money though because we would have to go as far away as possible because

Stuart's reach is wide. So, I started stealing money from Stuart and passing it to Ronnie to save for our future. It was a little at a time so he wouldn't suspect and Ronnie did his best to win at the card games he still attended."

I interrupt, saying incredulously, "Just how long has this, um, relationship been going on?"

Caroline looks down and mumbles, "Two years."

I stare at her in shock as my world crashes into shards of glass at my feet. Two years! Thinking back to when they started this, I picture a time when we were happy, weren't we? In fact, the more I think about it, our problems stemmed from that time and now I know why. Suddenly, I am facing the fact that my marriage was destroyed because of the person sitting before me innocently imploring me to understand and I feel like smashing something. It's all her fault.

I want to say so much but now I must hear her out because there's a sting to this tale that concerns me. Otherwise she wouldn't be here.

"We got careless." Her eyes are now wild and frantic and I can see the fear returning. "I took more money in the vain hope we could escape faster. Ronnie also got careless and we were almost caught a few times when he visited me at home." I feel sick and don't really want to hear anymore, but she carries on, regardless. "Then, one night, Stuart confronted me. He told me he knew I was stealing from him and hit me really badly. He was out of control and I was scared for my life. I ran and went to the one place I felt safe, The Blue Star."

"The pub, the one I saw you at when I was out with Ronnie?"

She nods. "I swear it was a coincidence that you were there at the same time, but Ronnie saw me sitting there when he went to the bar. He couldn't believe what I told him and was angry because of what Stuart did. He wanted us to leave, but I told him we had to wait. We were fools, Mrs Carter. We should have gone that day, but I thought it would blow over – it got worse."

Slumping back in my seat, I remember back to that time. We were trying again; we were going to make it work. Ronnie wanted a baby and to move to the North of England. What was that all about?

Caroline continues. "I bluffed my way out of it and told Stuart I needed the money for a gambling habit. I thought he believed me, but I should have known. He started to watch me – carefully. Soon he found out I wasn't acting alone, and that's when he discovered Ronnie's betrayal. The night Ronnie left you was the night Stuart left looking for him. To be honest, I'm not sure if they found him or not because I haven't heard a word from him since."

"They?" She looks at me in surprise and I say bitterly, "You said, they, who went to find Ronnie?"

She looks uncomfortable. "I'm sorry, Mrs Carter, but Stuart is not the sort of man you want to cross. He is a hard man and doesn't operate inside the law.

He's violent and runs things way worse than a gambling den and I'm afraid for Ronnie's life."

Now I feel distinctly nauseous and say weakly, "Do you think they found Ronnie?"

She nods. "That's what I'm afraid of. But I must also warn you that they may not have, and this is one of the places they will look for him. Make sure you're nowhere near here when they come knocking."

Like a dart piercing my heart, the fear returns. I think about the shadowy figure I believe is watching me. I feel the uncertainty as I walk down the street, as if someone is following me. In this moment, I know Caroline is right to be afraid and it's just a matter of time before they come knocking.

I look at her with suspicion and say roughly, "Why are you telling me this? Do you think I know where he is and will tell you because I don't and even I did, I wouldn't tell you?"

She nods. "I understand. You're angry and I don't blame you. No, I've made my own bed, Mrs Carter, and it's up to me to live with the consequences. I just wanted to right a wrong before an innocent person got hurt."

She stands and says fearfully. "I should go. If they are watching you, they will know I'm here. Don't hate me, Mrs Carter, because I didn't mean for any of this to happen. I just don't want to see you caught up in the fallout."

She heads to the door and I make no attempt to stop or even thank her because I can't wait for her to leave. As she reaches the front door, she turns and smiles apologetically, "I really loved Ronnie, you have to believe that and I never intended on hurting you. If you do see him, please..."

"Just go."

My voice is angry and I feel my blood boiling as she nods. "Of course. I'm sorry."

I watch her leave and then bolt the door and pull the curtains and feel my heart beating erratically as I replay her words in my mind. The fear inside me is almost too much to deal with as I picture Ronnie out there alone and afraid. Thinking of the money upstairs, it leaves a bitter taste in my mouth. It was *their* money. For *their* future and I don't want a penny of it. First thing tomorrow I am taking the lot and giving it to charity because then at least it will do some good, where it has done nothing but destroy so far.

26

The next day I drop the money in an envelope through the door of the local charity shop. I feel a great sense of satisfaction doing something that will help somebody else, which makes me feel a little better as I head off to the office.

From now on I am going to immerse myself in my job and look for a new place to rent because I can't stay in that house a minute longer.

Luckily, Julian is tied up with a lot of morning meetings that don't include me and I have time to register with a few lettings agencies and plan my move. I continue to research his wife and keep an eye on the comings and goings of Mr Slater by way of befriending his personal assistant Louise. In fact, I enjoy a nice chat with her at the coffee machine, where she reveals how much she despises her boss and wish he would leave already.

After arranging to meet her for lunch, I head back to my desk and carry on with my cyber stalking.

Just before 12.30, Julian calls me in and greets me with his customary, "Sit."

Maybe it's because of what happened yesterday, or maybe because I'm feeling irritable, I snap, "Please."

He raises his eyes and I see a storm approaching. "I beg your pardon."

My voice is tight as I reply, "Sit, please, would be a much nicer form of greeting."

He shakes his head and his eyes narrow, "Are you challenging me, Emma?"

I stand my ground. "I am."

"Why now?"

"Because I've had enough."

"Of what exactly?"

"Of being treated like dirt under your shoe. Of being spoken down to and of being made to feel as if I don't matter. I've had enough of being treated like a second-class citizen and if you don't like it, you only have yourself to blame."

I know I've gone too far when he hisses, "Firstly, I'll do whatever the fuck I like in my office. Secondly, you haven't earned the right to make demands on me after just a few weeks. Thirdly, I don't take kindly to being pulled up by my staff and fourthly…"

He breaks off and looks out of the window, seemingly thinking about whatever number four is, and I stand fully expecting my P45 to be slammed on the desk.

He turns around and says in a much softer voice, "And fourthly, please sit down, Emma."

I stare at him in shock and he nods. "I always listen to my staff and if I think they have a point, I'll admit to being in the wrong."

"You do?" I say it in surprise because I've never seen that for myself. He nods. "Yes, I'm fully aware of my own shortcomings and it takes a brave person to point them out. You are right to challenge me, which is why I apologise and ask you to, please sit down."

I do as he says and he smiles and in doing so, changes before my eyes. Gone is the surly, bad tempered, sex god and its place is a man who is magnificent in every way. I just stare open-mouthed because he laughs softly, "It's good that I've surprised you. I wondered how long it would take before you snapped."

"This was a test?"

My voice sounds disbelieving and he laughs. "Not really. I am an irritable bastard with no manners for most of the time, what can I say, they let me get away with it."

I just stare at him and he says firmly, "Anyway, I called you in to say we need to prepare the Zimmerman file. I'm meeting with him tomorrow and need all the data filled in to date and the action points from our last meeting, dotted and crossed. Can I leave that with you?"

"Of course, sir."

He nods and I take that as my cue to leave. As I stand, he says roughly, "A coffee would be good first."

He winks and turns back to his computer, leaving me in total shock. He winked. He actually winked as if he was joking with me. He said sorry and winked. I feel as if I'm in a parallel universe as I walk to the kitchen. What just happened? That was so unexpected. He must be playing a game, surely.

As arranged, I meet Louise for lunch in Barrington's and it feels good to come back here as a paying customer. It feels right to come here now after having avoided it for so long. I no longer feel ashamed of my old life and feel as if I should remember where I came from to keep my feet firmly on the ground because this life is likely to destroy me in a heartbeat if I let it.

Leah looks impressed as I place our order and as Louise grabs us a seat by the window, she whispers, "Look at you, hun. You look amazing, how's it going?"

"Good thanks, what about you, how is life here without me?"

Her brow furrows and I look at her with concern as she whispers, "Calvin is behaving really weird lately."

"Why, he seemed ok when I came in last time?"

Looking around, she says, "Hailey left and wouldn't say why. She was angry with Calvin for some reason and ever since then, he's been like a bear with a sore head."

"What do you think happened?"

She shrugs and pours the steamed milk on top of the coffee. "It's anyone's guess, but there's no talking to him. It's left me in the lurch though because he hasn't even replaced her, saying she'll cool down and will back soon."

"You don't think…"

She nods. "Yes, I do think. You know Calvin, he's always been a bit of a letch and free with his hands. I'm guessing he was a little improper with Hailey and she's left for that reason."

My heart sinks as I think that Leah is probably right. Calvin was always a little overfamiliar and had to be put in his place a few times. Both Leah and I were quite vocal about it, so he got the message and left us alone. Hailey was always a little more bashful and wouldn't say boo to a goose. She would put up with anything, which makes me angry when I think of what he must have done to her.

Leah looks annoyed. "If I didn't need this job, I'd leave, but then I feel as if I need to warn his next victim. Why do men have to be so… sleazy?"

"I don't know, it's wrong though. If I were you, I'd keep an account of it all in case…"

"In case what?" Leah's eyes are wide and I smile reassuringly. "No reason, just in case questions are asked."

She nods and after I pay, I head across to Louise who smiles sweetly. "Thanks, Emma. You know, this is nice. I can't think why we haven't done this before."

"Me too. I suppose we're always at the beck and call of our masters."

She pulls a face and makes a gagging sound. "At least yours is eye candy of the best kind."

"Yes, with a very sour taste when you bite into it."

She giggles and says wistfully, "I wouldn't mind a bite."

We laugh and then she leans forward. "Have you… I mean, taken a bite?"

I look at her in shock. "Of course not, why, is that usual?"

She looks a little flushed and I say incredulously, "Have you?"

"Oh god no, I wish, it's just that…"

Suddenly, she looks worried and I think back to her own boss and say softly, "Mr Slater?"

She nods and looks a little upset and then says quickly, "It's ok, I wanted to, at least I did back then but now I actually know him, he doesn't seem so attractive to me anymore."

I feel sick as I think of the vile man preying on the pretty girl before me and looking across at Leah say with sadness, "Is this common, I mean, the boss messing around with his staff?"

Louise shrugs and takes a sip of her coffee. "I don't think so. I mean, I've never heard of Mr Landon being indiscreet."

Thinking back to the flush on Harriet's cheeks, I'm not so sure, and suddenly, I feel sick to my stomach. All of this - it sickens me. Men using women for their willingness to get ahead and women for allowing it to happen. Suddenly, I'm tired. Tired of it all. This isn't what I thought it was going to be and now I'm not so sure I want to be a part of this world, in fact, any world when getting ahead is all that matters.

Thinking of what I've done myself to sit where I am now, fills me with shame. This isn't me; when did I become this person I am now, scheming and plotting just to get a smile of approval from an extremely complicated man?

Louise looks concerned. "Are you ok, Emma? You've gone a little pale."

Smiling with a reassurance I don't feel, I say lightly, "I'm fine thanks. Anyway, tell me about life in Slater's office. I'm guessing it's much the same as mine."

I listen as Louise babbles on about how demanding her boss is, and I feel so weary. Why did I ever want to become part of this nest of vipers? The trouble is, it's all crumbling around me and I don't have many options.

What on earth am I going do next?

27

I'm so happy when I can call it a night and head home. Although the rest of the day passed without a hitch, I feel differently now. The job no longer seems exciting and just leaves a bad taste in my mouth and has left with it a feeling of uncertainty. I know I can't go back to my old job; I've moved on a lot since then, but what next?

My mind is so tied up in knots, it takes me a moment to register that things are different when I head inside my front door, but as my eyes adjust; the fear grips me.

Somebody's been here.

It's not apparent, but I know. Drawers and cupboards are left slightly open where I always shut them properly, it's a particular gripe of mine with Ronnie who never closes anything. The cushions have been rearranged as if somebody has been searching for something and I just know that the house has been searched.

Immediately, I race upstairs to our bedroom and see evidence of a search there as well. Was it Ronnie? Did he come back for more things - the money?

Quickly, I move from room to room and see things out of place and my heart sinks. Whoever was here obviously didn't find what they were looking for, which means it couldn't be Ronnie unless it was the money he was after. He may have thought I hid it somewhere else and went looking. The trouble is, I don't think it could have been him because why wouldn't he just call and ask for it? Then again, he may be fearful of recriminations after what he did.

Thinking of Ronnie makes me sad. How did it all go so badly wrong? Why start an affair when things were good at home because they were? It's only the last couple of years that things changed and now I know why. His letter begged me not to hate him, but how can I not? He has destroyed what we had and there's no going back.

Then I think about the man who is after him, and my heart beats a little faster. If it was him, he may be back when I'm home and beat it out of me. Suddenly, I realise what a dangerous situation I'm in and my heart sinks and my knees tremble. I need to leave, but where?

I'm not sure why I even thought it was a good idea, but I reach for my phone and dial the number I should avoid at all costs. Even as I listen to it ring, I know I've made a big mistake, but something is telling me it's the only solution. "What is it?"

His tone is as harsh as always and yet somehow the tears fall for a different reason his time.

With a break to my voice, I stutter, "I'm sorry, Julian, I'm in trouble."

Immediately, I sense a change in tone as he says urgently. "Where are you?"

The tears refuse to stay hidden and I sob, "At home, but somebody's been here."

"I'll be right there."

He cuts the call and I sob with relief because if I need anyone right now, it's my boss because I need a man of action and he is the sort who will get results and fast.

Wrapping my arms around me, I cry hard for the life I lost and the man that went with it. I cry for my own actions of the past few months and the broken dreams I held so high. I cry for the woman in me who thought she could do better, and I cry for the fact I'm so tired of it all.

It must be thirty minutes later, a loud banging on my door brings me to my feet and I hold my breath as I fear the reason for it. What if it's Stuart and his thugs come to claim what's theirs but then I hear a terse, "For God's sake, Emma open the bloody door."

The relief hits me hard as I stumble towards it and as I fling it open, I stare at the man I love to hate and the tears fall fast. He looks shocked and for some reason, his first instinct is to pull me towards him and wrap his arms around me, saying softly, "It's ok, you're safe now."

Strangely, it doesn't feel wrong being in his arms in the home I shared with Ronnie, which surprises me more than anything. He pulls away a little and says gently, "Tell me what happened."

"The house, someone has been here. They're searching for something and may come back."

He looks around and says in surprise, "It looks ok to me."

Feeling a little foolish, I shake my head and say weakly, "It's a long story."

Closing the door behind him, he takes my hand and pulls me into the living room and forces me to sit on the faded settee we've had for close on five years.

Sitting beside me, he takes my hand and squeezes it gently and says in a surprisingly gentle voice, "Then you had better start at the beginning."

In a monotone voice, I tell him everything. About Ronnie, the arguments, the fact he left me and then Caroline's visit and the story she told. When I reach the end, he shakes his head in amazement. "That's a lot to deal with on your own."

I nod miserably and he says firmly, "You can't stay here, it's not safe. Come, you can stay at the house tonight and then we'll discuss a more permanent solution tomorrow."

"But…" he places his finger on my lips and says with a hint of steel in his voice. "Don't argue with me, Emma, and just do as you're told. I'm not taking no for an answer. Grab your things and I mean enough for a month and we will make sure everything is sorted.

He pulls me up and I allow myself to be ordered around as I'm used to by now. It doesn't take me long to pack a couple of suitcases and as he loads them into his car, I take a long, lingering look at the house that holds so many memories.

Then I turn the key on my past and walk towards an uncertain future.

28

We stay silent for the journey and I think I must be in shock because I can't stop shaking. Julian turns up the heater on his car and plays some soft music, and I allow him to take charge. It feels nice to be cared for after the last few months, where I have been so alone and as we speed through the night, I wish we could stay like this forever.

When we arrive at Julian's impressive home, he drives to a separate building set behind his large mansion.

"This is the guest house, it's yours for the night. You should find everything you need and what you don't have, Nicola will fetch for you."

As I look around Julian's guest house, I am blown away. It's bigger than my actual house and much grander. It's modern, clean and comfortable and has everything a girl could ever wish for.

Even the kitchen is stocked and he flings open the fridge and nods his approval. "Good, I called ahead and told Nicola to make sure there were supplies.

As he turns around, I say in a whisper, "Thank you."

His face looks different somehow, more relaxed, less stressed, and his eyes are bright as he smiles with a kindness I rarely see in him. "You're welcome. I'm just glad you called."

"Are you?" There is surprise in my voice and he nods.

"Believe it or not, Emma, I care about you. I care about your personal safety and would hate to see anything happen to you."

He laughs at the disbelief that must show on my face and heads across, once again taking my hand and leading me to a comfortable settee in a light airy room.

"When I first met you, the day you walked uninvited into my office, I was interested. Nobody had ever done anything like that before and you had balls – I liked it. Even when I tore you down, you had a strength to you that impressed me, unlike the usual victims of my acid tongue who crumbled before my eyes. Over the past few weeks, you have risen to the challenge and worked hard and without question. I am very demanding – I know that, and yet you coped when you had no experience. So, you see, Emma, I think you might just be the strongest woman I have ever met and when you called today with fear in your voice, I knew it had to be something bad. So, don't thank me because I owe you this one at least. Just settle in knowing you are safe and tomorrow we will deal with the situation."

He stands. "Ok, I'll leave you to it. Meet me by my car at 7am. Tomorrow looks to be a busy day."

As he leaves, I stare at the door he left through for a very long time. He has surprised me – again. One minute I hate him with every fibre of my being and want to throttle him on the spot. Then he does something so lovely I think I fall in love with him a little more. Love and hate are balancing a very fine line here, which makes me think about his marriage. Does Cressida have the same feelings towards him? Does she love him fiercely and with passion and want to kill him the next?

Uncomfortable at the way my thoughts are heading, I distract myself by exploring their lovely home. I feel a pang of envy as I register the rich, expensive furniture that I doubt gets much use. The tasteful accessories that look to have cost more than I have made in my lifetime dazzle me. The sheer decadence of having a home within a home and a place for guests to stay away from the main house is the impossible dream and it feels as if nothing can touch me here and I am safe in a little corner of paradise.

7am and I wait beside Julian's car with my teeth chattering. It's a frosty morning and I have just a thin coat. Blowing on my hands, I wish for the umpteenth time that he would hurry up and keep stealing looks towards the house, praying for the large wooden door to open. After ten minutes waiting, I begin to think he is doing this on purpose and watching me freeze is just another one of his sadistic games.

Finally, my prayers are answered and the door opens and my heart flutters as he jogs down the steps in a padded coat, looking so hot I feel the warmth thaw me instantly.

Clicking the lock on his car, he says abruptly, "Get in."

No 'Good morning, I trust you slept well.' Just the terse orders of a man with no polite conversation.

I need no further invitation and sit shivering in the seat, desperate for the heater to start working as a matter of urgency.

As he starts the engine and waits for the frost to melt off the screen, he plugs in his phone and says in a deep voice, "We have a busy day today, Emma. We are falling behind and I need to catch up. There are to be no distractions today."

I say nothing as he moves the car away from his impressive home and we start the journey to work. It doesn't take long for the heated seats to warm my frozen bones and as the heater gets to work on my feet, I relax in the comfort of a powerful sports car. This car, like the man who drives it, cuts through life with power and command. It overtakes the slower, less able machines and roars past, shoving them firmly in their place behind it. I can see why people desire such objects because as aphrodisiacs go, money is a powerful one. However, I am fast realising you pay with your soul and I'm not prepared to do that anymore.

Thirty minutes into the journey, Julian says, "Regarding the break in at your home."

My heart leaps and I whisper nervously, "What about it?"

"I spent the night looking into what you told me. I've instructed an investigator I use to look into it and report back. I've given him the details of your husband, the man after him, and your address. I just wanted to let you know it's in hand and not to think of it."

I feel weak with relief and a warm feeling spreads over me. It feels good that he's helping and it makes me warm to him even more, but then he says roughly, "I can't have you distracted from my business. It's most irritating and we don't have time for it."

"Excuse me?" I know I sound hurt and annoyed and he snaps, "Deal with it, Emma because I hired you to do a job. Your personal life cannot distract you from what I've employed you to do. I know what women are like and you won't be able to think of anything else. Your work will suffer and you'll be of no use to me."

I feel the rage twist the knot that sits inside me and say tightly, "God forbid I would let my own problems interfere with yours. You know, Julian, last night I thought I saw a glimmer of hope that you were actually human. I revised my opinion of you because you were so kind. Now I can see it was just for your own reasons, and I can't believe I was so stupid to think that you actually had a heart. Well, for your information, I have lived with this situation, as you call it, for quite a while now and it hasn't once stopped me from doing my job. So, just fuck off, Julian and give me just a little credit and allow me to upset that my home was broken into and some crazy criminal is out to get me. I know that may irritate you and get in the way of your plans, but hard luck, it can't be helped. What can I say, life's a bitch and you should know more about that than most of us because you're the biggest bitch in the life of everyone that knows you?"

His laughter stops me in my tracks and I shout, "Are you laughing at me?"

"Of course."

"Why, of course?"

"Because you amuse me, Emma. I love winding you up, it's so easy and helps pass the time. You see, I can read you like a book and you never disappoint me. You know, car sharing is such fun, don't you agree?"

"Stupid prick."

I murmur my response and look out of the window, and Julian just laughs even more. However, the mood in the car has lifted a little and I turn away so he can't see the smile on my lips. For all his attitude, I kind of like sparring with him. Now I understand a little of how he ticks, I don't feel a fraction of the hurt his words are designed to inflict. Once again, I realise how far I've fallen if I think this is acceptable and once again, decide that the sooner I get another job and leave this madness behind, the better.

29

Julian wasn't wrong. We have fallen behind and the day rushes past in work, more work, followed by even more work. He is rude, demanding and irritable and I rush around like a headless chicken with a head filled with facts, figures and deadlines. I've lost count of the files I located for him and the calls I've made to set up meetings and book restaurants. I've made more coffee than a man should surely have the ability to stand and turned more people away than ever before, much to their disgust.

The day passes in a blur and soon the memory of the sandwiches I grabbed from the canteen at lunchtime are a distant memory. 7pm comes and I am on my knees. I am tired, hungry and mentally exhausted, which is actually a good thing because I haven't thought about my own problems all day. There hasn't been time and as I shut down my computer, it suddenly strikes me that I was only allowed one night at Julian's guest house and I feel the fear returning as I wonder if he expects me to return home.

Then again, my things are still at his guest house, so I'm not so sure.

He interrupts my thoughts by heading my way with a terse, "Get your coat."

I quickly do as he says and follow him, as usual ten steps behind, as he races for the lift.

Once inside, he punches the button angrily and runs his fingers through his hair, the only indication that he, like me, is exhausted.

Feeling his eyes on me, I glance up and see a storm in his eyes and swallow hard as he says, "You look hungry, we'll grab something on the way."

"Where are we going?"

"Home, of course."

Feeling a little silly, I say, "What, my home?"

"Of course not, don't be obtuse, *my* home. I told you that you weren't going back there until it's sorted."

I feel weak with relief and it must show because he says in a softer voice. "We don't have time for your problems, so it suits me that you stay close to hand. The guest house is yours until further notice while we deal with what's important."

"Which is?" I already know the answer but want the bastard to voice it for once, which he appears happy to do. "The most important thing at the moment, Emma, is me. The most important thing in the foreseeable future, is me. So, you see, you could be staying for some time because I always put myself and my family first and until I have no further use for you, you will do what's best – for me."

I stare at him with so much hate flashing from my eyes, I see the spark burn brighter in his. It's as if he feeds off hatred and it makes him stronger. He doesn't wait for an answer because the lift stops and once again, I am running after him, struggling to keep up.

It's as if he has me on an invisible thread and is pulling me after him at speed. I am bouncing along behind him hitting the deck, getting bruised and battered and fearing for my life because he is relentless, cruel and a bully and yet has this ability to keep you wanting more.

I try not to make conversation with him on the journey home and look up in surprise as he pulls to a stop outside a smart restaurant on the outskirts of London.

A valet is waiting to take his car and park it and he says in a commanding voice, "Let's eat."

Wearily, I follow him from the car, once again, opening my own door and stepping out onto the cold pavement by the side of a welcoming, warmly lit, restaurant. The place is alive and appears bursting at the seams and I feel the warmth of a place that holds so much promise. For my stomach, anyway.

The waiter shows us to a reserved table, once again in the window and looks to be the best seat in the house and I say in surprise, "When did you book this?"

He shrugs. "Just before we left."

As I look around, it strikes me that the restaurant is full and yet we have the best table. They are turning people away and yet only thirty minutes ago he called to reserve a table. Once again, I understand the power of money and I feel a bad taste in my mouth. It shouldn't be this way. How will men like Julian ever be better people if they are allowed to get away with it?

The waiter stands beside us politely waiting for instruction and once again, Julian rattles off our requirements with no regard for what I want. As the waiter nods, I say loudly, "Actually, can I change mine and have a gin and tonic and a plate of your house pasta with a green salad, please, if it's not too much trouble."

The waiter looks at Julian a little nervously and he barks, "Well, you heard the lady give her what she wants."

Backing away, the waiter heads off and I say crossly, "Did you have to be so rude?"

"Did you?"

"Me, are you kidding, how was it rude to ask for something I actually want?"

"Because I know best and you were just showing off."

"Me - showing off – says the man who shows off for most of the day. Honestly, Julian, you are such an idiot. In fact, I can't believe you've actually got this far in life not knowing it."

His hand moves so fast I don't see it coming and he pulls me towards him so quickly the table decoration almost goes flying. His mouth is inches from mine as he whispers, "I love the fire in you, Emma. I want to taste it for myself. I want to take your lips in mine and devour them. I want you more than I've wanted anyone before and the more you resist me, the more I want you."

My heart is pounding so hard, I'm fearful I'm about to have a cardiac arrest as my body responds to the man I love to hate. My breath hitches as his eyes glitter dangerously before me and it takes everything in me to say in a frosty voice, "Let me go."

Immediately, he releases me and I sit back in my chair and take a few deep breaths, as I struggle to make sense of what just happened. I almost can't look at him as he raises his glass to me and says in a deep, husky voice, "I always get what I want, Emma, it's only a matter of time."

I'm not sure if he's referring to what just happened, or the fact he wants to destroy his wife, but I choose to ignore him. Instead, I concentrate on my food that arrives quickly and just eat, trying to regain some sort of control over myself.

Julian decides that conversation is no longer required and we eat our meal in peace as he taps on his phone for much of it. However, there is an undercurrent of something building that can only result in one thing, and I'm not sure I'm prepared for it.

30

Despite everything that's happened, I settle into life at Julian's guest house and soon it becomes like my own home. Every time I broach the subject of leaving, Julian comes up with more reasons why I should stay and we soon settle into a routine where we share the journey to and from work and occasionally grab something to eat on the way back.

On the evenings Julian eats with his family, Nicola prepares the same meal for me, which is delivered to the guest house and waiting when I return.

If I'm lonely, it doesn't feel like it because this little bubble I've fallen into is just what I need right now after the trauma of the past few months.

Julian is also a little less angry, less demanding and a surprisingly good companion when he wants to be, pushing my desire to leave even further away.

There is still no word about Ronnie, but Julian assures me he is working on it and I have to be satisfied with that. I dread what they may find, anyway, so carry on being cared for in a world far away from the one I was brought up in.

I don't set foot inside the main house, which suits me fine because the thought of coming face to face with Cressida is not a pleasant one. However, I am curious to know what she thinks of me staying here but am not brave enough to raise the subject.

So, it's with some surprise that as I wait for Julian by his car at 7am, he opens the main front door and beckons me over.

"Emma, you will work from here today."

Quickly, I move towards him and note that he appears tired and irritated and my heart sinks. This could prove to be a very trying day.

As I enter his home, he says tersely, "Come, I have a very special job for you today."

Instead of heading to his study, he heads into the drop dead, gorgeous kitchen and I stare in surprise at the two pretty little girls sitting at the island unit, eating their cereal in their pyjamas,

They look at me shyly and Julian says in a softer voice than normal, "Girls, this is Emma. She works for daddy and will be looking after you today."

I stare at him in total shock and he shakes his head, warning me from saying anything.

I look back at the girls who look interested and smile pleasantly. Then one says, "Hi, Emma, I like your shoes."

Looking down at my red stilettos, I laugh. "Thank you very much…"

She grins. "Amelia." Turning to her sister, she says sweetly, "This is Imogen and she's shy."

Imogen blushes prettily and looks down and I say softly, "There's nothing wrong with being shy. Did you know that when I was Imogen's age, I used to ask my friend to speak for me? I couldn't bear to speak because I didn't want anyone to look at me."

Imogen looks up under her lashes with curiosity and I move across and sit beside them. "We all have something special about us and I can see that you are both very special girls in different ways. We can't all be the same, and that's absolutely fine. So, Amelia, Imogen, I understand we will be spending the day together, is that ok with you?"

Amelia nods vigorously while Imogen stares at her cereal. "What are we going to do, Emma, can we play fairy camps?"

Laughing, I nod. "That sounds like fun. You will have to show me how it's done though because it's a long time since I was a fairy." Amelia looks pleased and Julian interrupts, "A word, Emma."

My heart sinks as I make my way across the room, leaving the two girls to carry on eating, and he whispers, "Nicola's on a day off and Cressida didn't come home last night. I can't watch them all day, and so I'll work from home while you entertain them. If Cressida shows up, we're off the hook."

I nod and he says tersely, "I'll be in my study. Give them whatever they want and keep them out of my way."

He strides off and I feel so angry I can hardly speak and hoping they didn't hear a word he just said, I smile brightly and say, "Right then, can I get you anything else to eat?"

Amelia says loudly, "Chocolate." Imogen giggles. Laughing, I reach for an apple from the overflowing fruit bowl and cut it into pieces with a knife resting in a block by the kettle. "In our house this was considered the finest chocolate."

Amelia laughs. "That's just a stupid old apple."

"To you, maybe. But where I come from, it's the finest food imaginable."

They look doubtful and I lean on the counter and take a piece of apple and pop in my mouth, groaning with pleasure. They stare at me in astonishment as I savour every morsel and say in a whisper, "Don't tell anyone I told you, but this is what princesses eat to make them beautiful and strong. They eat at least three a day because this is magic food."

Even Imogen looks interested as Amelia gasps, "I want some."

Shaking my head, I pop another slice into my mouth and watch as they suddenly decide they want this apple more than any packet of chocolate they may have in the cupboard. I finish and say sternly, "Only people who understand its power can eat it. If they don't, it doesn't work, you see, magic apple, like I said, is more powerful than anything else. It makes you grow big and strong. It gives you the power to fight off anything that may harm you. Your hair grows long and shiny and your teeth sparkle. Chocolate destroys all its good work and was created by evil witches who want to control you. Are you strong enough for the power of the apple?"

Amelia nods vigorously and Imogen nods slowly. "Then I will grant your wish and let you sample the power yourself."

Quickly, I cut them each a slice and offer it to them both solemnly. They take it in their hands as if it's the finest jewel and take little bites out of the end. I see the excitement in their eyes as they devour it and laugh to myself as they look at each other with pride and joy. Then Amelia jumps up and runs around the room, shouting, "I've got the power. Come on Imo, let's go and get our fairy dresses on."

Laughing, I make to follow them and then hear a soft laugh and turn to see Julian leaning on the door frame, shaking his head. "Stupid kids, they believe anything."

Feeling annoyed for them, I say, "Stupid father, doesn't see the true value of what he has."

Then I walk after them, leaving him standing there with a strange look on his face.

31

I am utterly exhausted. I can't believe children have so much energy.

I followed them to their room, which actually turned out to be an entire floor of the house. They each have their own amazing rooms and a shared playroom that is larger than my entire upstairs at home. It is stuffed with every toy imaginable and decorated in the prettiest pastel pinks. The carpet is totally impractical for children and is the softest, deepest white, with scatter rugs everywhere. I am completely blown away by how much these two girls have and feel a little sad as I see it's just to make up for the fact they have two parents who don't want to spend time with them.

Nicola was right, these girls are lovely in every way and now I know why she stays here. They are good company and I'm happy to see that Imogen begins to relax and comes out of her shell a little, as she lives under the shadow of her more outspoken sister.

We decide to head to the kitchen for lunch and I allow them to help me make some sandwiches and more apples than is probably good for them. I find some little cakes in a tin that I decide will do as a treat if they eat all their sandwiches and fruit. I even make one for Julian, although I'm tempted to get him to make his own, but a part of me wants him to eat with his children because I'm guessing they don't do that very often.

So, as the girls wash their hands as instructed, I head towards his study and knock tentatively on the door.

"Come in."

As usual, his voice is irritable and I head inside and see him staring at the computer with a deep frown. "What do you want?"

"Lunch is ready and we thought it would be nice if you joined us."

He looks up in surprise. "Lunch, already, why what's the time?"

"12."

He looks at his watch and groans. "Fuck, I haven't stopped."

He stands and then looks a little anxious. "Have they behaved themselves?"

I can't help the smile that breaks out across my face as I nod. "They are amazing, you should be very proud."

His face softens just for a minute and then he moves towards the door. "Ten minutes, then I must get back to work."

Sighing, I follow him to the kitchen where the girls are waiting, eyeing up the apple keenly. Julian laughs as Amelia says seriously, "Daddy, you can have the sandwiches and we can have the apple."

Grabbing a stool beside her, he ruffles her hair and says seriously, "It doesn't work like that. You see, the apple needs the sandwich to activate its power. Without the balance it won't work."

Amelia groans. "Why is life so complicated?"

Julian laughs loudly and tickles her relentlessly, and as she giggles and screams, I stare at him in astonishment. Who is this man?

He turns his attention to Imogen and lifts her onto his knee and strokes her hair softly, kissing the top of her head and feeding her a little bite of a sandwich.

Suddenly, everything shifts in my world. I see him properly for the first time, and I like it very much. Now I see the man behind the sharp retorts and cutting remarks. In his own home, surrounded by the people he loves – and he does love them, it's plain to see – he becomes much more of a man in my eyes and now I'm more than interested.

Lunch is very different to how I imagined it to be. Ten minutes turns to twenty and we laugh more than we eat. The girls entertain us with stories from school, and I'm glad to see that Imogen opens up a little and interjects with tales of her own.

Therefore, it's like a cold bucket of water soaks us to the skin when we hear a cool, "Well, isn't this nice?"

Immediately, the humour leaves the room and I watch as Julian reverts back to the cold bastard he is for most of the time. The girls look down and start eating and I turn to stare at the beautiful woman, in looks alone, who glides into the room, very much looking like the queen of all she surveys.

Julian snaps, "Good of you to show up."

Cressida shrugs and looks at me pointedly. "What's that?"

She waves a well-manicured finger in my direction and Julian says with an ice-laden voice, "Go to my study, Emma."

Feeling like a fish out of water, I do as he says because I am, quite honestly, keen to get away from this vicious woman. I hear him say in a softer tone, "Girls, go and choose one of your favourite films to watch while daddy talks with mummy."

Even they leave with no words spoken, and it strikes me that they didn't seem pleased to see their mother at all. I thought they would run into her arms, or squeal with delight, but her appearance just dampened the atmosphere.

As I wait in Julian's study, I can only wonder what they are saying and if I feel anything, it's pity for those poor little girls who are such a credit to their parents.

I take a seat in the corner and shrivel up inside. What's that? Her words haunt me as I replay them over and over in my mind. Those two words made me feel so worthless, so unimportant, and as if I didn't matter in the slightest. I feel cheap and as if I am worth nothing and it hurts.

The tears slide down my face and I brush them angrily away. I'm a nobody, the grey woman who watches everyone else have a life. My place is in the shadows where nobody has to look at me because I am not one of them. Even Ronnie didn't want me, and my own family couldn't care. I have no friends and no life outside of work, which I hate more and more every day.

What's that? I can't get the words out of my mind as I lose it completely. Why do I even bother trying? I should know my place and should never have dared to think I was someone better than I am.

I'm not sure how long I sit in the chair in the corner. Time has no meaning anymore because obviously I don't count. I am made to wait for someone else to tell me what happens next with my own life, and I am so defeated I sit patiently waiting for it to happen. 'What's that' just about sums my life up and I feel empty inside.

Then Julian heads into the room and looks so angry I can almost taste it.

He doesn't even glance in my direction as he snaps, "We're leaving."

Once again, I run after him as he heads through his house and wrenches the front door open.

I struggle to keep up as he heads to his car and just about manage to fasten my seatbelt before he screeches out of the drive, leaving the gravel shooting off in all directions.

He is so angry I wonder if this was such a good idea being in the car with him at all because he drives like a madman down the country roads that lead away from his palatial home.

He doesn't speak at all until we screech to a halt in an underground car park and then turns to me and says tersely, "Come."

For the first time, I speak, "Where are we?"
"You'll see."

He exits the car and heads towards an elevator in the corner, and I hurry to catch him up as he locks the car behind me. As we wait for the lift, he taps his foot angrily on the concrete floor and growls, "I've had enough. That bitch is going to get what she deserves and I will deliver it personally."

I don't think I've ever seen him so angry and daren't speak as we enter the lift and the only sound I can hear is the machinery starting up as it propels us to God only knows where.

We arrive at what appears to be an office complex and he strides down a carpeted hallway towards a door at the end. The name on the door is, 'Smith & Robinson' and I wonder what they do.

The woman on the reception desk nods as she sees Julian and says pleasantly, "Mr Landon, it's good to see you. Go straight through."

We don't even sign in and Julian strides towards a door at the end and knocks loudly. I hear a pleasant voice shout, "Julian, good to see you," and then the door slams in my face. Feeling a little shaken, I turn around and take a seat in what appears to be a small waiting room and try to grab what's left of my dignity around me.

32

Once again, I wait alone, feeling worthless and as if I don't count. I'm of half a mind to walk out of the door and never look back, but I have nowhere to go. My life has unravelled so quickly I never saw it coming and I feel the despair overwhelming me and sink my head into my hands. A lone tear slides down my face and splashes onto my skirt, and I cry bitterly on the inside. I can't break down; I need to stay strong because I'm all I've got.

I don't hear the door open and the first thing I'm aware of is a strong arm pulling me close to a familiar scent. Those same arms lock me tight and his hand strokes my hair much like he did to his daughter and whispers, "It's ok, I've got you."

Pulling back, I wipe my tears away and feel foolish and weak. Everything he despises and try to pull myself together. "It's fine, I'm being stupid."

The look he is giving me is not his standard one and I sense something just happened in that room, because his eyes sparkle with an excitement I haven't seen for a while.

"What happened?" I am shocked out of my pit of despair and he pulls me to my feet and swings me around, leaving me more shocked than I was before.

"It's done and now we're going to celebrate."

I stare at him in disbelief, and then I hear a low chuckle coming from the corner of the room. Looking in the direction it's coming from, I see a portly man watching us, shaking his head with amusement. Julian actually smiles at the man and pulls me over to meet him. "Charles, this is Emma, my assistant."

Holding out his hand, Charles grips mine hard and shakes it vigorously. "I'm pleased to meet you; I've heard a lot about you."

"You have?" I stare at him in surprise, and then he turns to Julian and shakes his hand just as vigorously. "We'll iron out the details over the next 24 hours, so lie low for a couple of days. Maybe give us until Thursday and then it should be done."

Julian smiles and says gratefully, "I owe you big time for this."

Charles nods. "A bottle of my preferred tipple will do just fine."

Julian grins and grabs my hand and pulls me after him, and I don't mind in the slightest. Where I am normally running behind him struggling to keep up, this time he holds my hand firmly and walks beside me with an air of familiarity that doesn't escape my attention. What's happening?

As soon as we reach the lift and the doors close, he pulls me close and tilts my head back to look into his eyes. Then to my utter amazement, his lips crash against mine and he fists my hair, devouring my mouth as he pushes me hard against the walls. I'm not sure what on earth is happening, but I'm not complaining? Despite everything, I kiss him back with a desperate passion that has been building for months. We kiss like lovers and I groan as his hard body pushes into mine and I feel how interested he is in me all of a sudden.

The lift brings us back to earth with a bump and he grabs my hand again and almost runs with me to his waiting car.

This time, he holds the door open for me and sees me safely inside. This time, he fastens my seat belt with a care that warms my heart and then he kisses me softly on the lips and whispers huskily, "Now, let me show you how important you are."

I stare ahead of me in shock, as he jumps into the driver's seat and reverses at speed out of the space. Then he heads off through the traffic and I say with a stutter, "What's happening, where are we going?"

He grins. "You heard the man; we need to lie low for a couple of days. I'm taking you away with me."

"But where, why…?"

I am confused and he reaches over and grips my hand tightly. "Trust me, Emma. Soon it will all be done and we can start again."

"What are you talking about?" Suddenly, I feel nervous as I sense change coming. What does he mean, start again, will I lose my job and be out on the street?

"Charles is my lawyer and he's worked out the final settlement with Cressida. He has lodged files with her solicitor outlining the details of the divorce and she would be a fool to refuse."

"But what if she does, and why do we have to lie low? What about the girls, are they safe?"

"Nicola is back and has been instructed to watch over them. Cressida is probably currently reeling from the conversation I just had with her before we left. It's over, Emma, I've won as I always knew I would."

"But how and where does this leave me?"

"By my side, where you belong. I've been fighting this attraction since the moment I set eyes on you. It was bad timing and could have messed with my mind. So, I hired you to keep you close and now I can stop fighting it and see where it leads us."

"Don't I get a say in the matter?"

I ask but he's right. I can't refuse him anything and he knows it. Pulling over to the kerb, he cuts the engine and turns to look at me with the intense stare I am accustomed to. "Well?"

"Well what?

"You want your say, so hit me with it."

Now I have the opportunity to tell him exactly what I think of him, my words dry up. The way he is looking at me is what was in my dreams at night. The words he's spoken I've imagined in my head over and over again, and every sharp word and derogatory comment means nothing right now. So, I just shrug and look away. "You'll have to work a bit harder than this to make up for what you've put me through over the past few weeks."

He reaches out and takes my hand, raising it to his lips and kisses it softly. Then he lifts my hair away from my eyes and runs his thumb across my lips. "I want you, Emma, and I always get what I want. I told you, you intrigue me and these past few weeks have proved to me how strong you are. When I saw you with my daughters, it showed me the woman I was always meant to find. Strong, beautiful and kind with a softness that's irresistible to any man. So, Emma Carter, will you allow me to prove to you that you matter a great deal to me and forgive me for ever making you think otherwise?"

I can't resist him, as much as I am trying to, it's too much and so, I nod slowly and once again, his lips find mine and kiss me slowly, softly and as if he genuinely loves me. My heart flutters like in the movies and the last piece of the wall I have built between us, crumbles to dust. I can't fight him, it's impossible, so I give in to what my heart and body want and kiss him back with everything I've got.

33

I'm in love. I can't believe it's happened, but I actually love Julian Landon.

For the past two days we've been inseparable. We have stayed in a beautiful country hotel just outside London and haven't left the room. We've talked, slept and eaten amazing meals for two, delivered by room service in the best suite the hotel offers. We haven't dressed and have just worn dressing gowns and fed each other morsels of the finest food prepared by award-winning chefs.

We have made love for hours and explored each other until I feel as if I know every part of him. We've watched old movies and drank wine and talked long into the night.

How could I not fall in love with such a charismatic man and I don't think I have ever been as happy in my life?

Two days later, everything changes.

Julian's phone rings and as I walk into the room dripping from the shower, I see him answer it with a frown. The conversation is short, but the look he gives me tells me it's not a happy call. He says tersely, "Of course, we'll be right there."

"What is it?" My voice is anxious because the look in his eyes is scaring me. Reaching out, he pulls me close and wraps his arms around me, as if to protect me from what he's about to say.

"They've found your husband."

Grateful for his strength, I collapse against his body, my legs shaking so much I can hardly stand. "Ronnie." I whisper his name as if I can't believe it. "Where is he?"

He squeezes me tighter and says in a low voice, "I'm sorry, my darling."

"Sorry, what are you sorry about?"

I feel the hysteria rising and my voice comes out high and frightened. Pulling me next to him on the bed, he takes my hands and looks deep into my eyes. "I'm so sorry, he's dead."

"Dead?" I struggle to understand what he's saying and the tears just trickle from my eyes as my brain struggles to register what he's saying "Dead?" I whisper the word as if its meaning escapes me. "How?"

He strokes my hair and wipes the tears away, saying softly, "It appears that he was murdered."

That was the last thing I heard because I wake up lying on the bed with a cold flannel pressed to my forehead. Julian is stroking my head and whispering, "It's ok, Emma, let it sink in. Cry all you want."

I think I'm in shock because I can't even cry and just repeat, "Ronnie's dead?"

It must take a good ten minutes before I sit up and say in a broken voice, "How?"

"I don't know the details, but we need to attend the police station. They want to question you and they…"

"What?"

I feel frightened as he says with an edge to his voice, "They want you to formally identify the body."

Nodding, I make to stand and Julian says gently, "Do you need more time for it to sink in?"

"No." My voice is hoarse. "I must see for myself. I need to understand what happened."

As we get ready to leave, I feel as if I'm in a trance. Ronnie is dead, I can't believe it.

It doesn't take us long to reach the police station and we are shown to an interview room where the detective in charge of the case is waiting. Julian sits beside me and I'm grateful for that because inside I'm a mess and am struggling to take it all in.

The detective arranges for some tea, for the shock I think, and tells us what he knows already.

"We were called to a park on the west side of town where a dog walker reported a body floating in the nearby river. We recovered it and found a man who we believe to be your husband, floating face down with severe stab wounds to his chest and neck."

I think I'm going to be sick and Julian squeezes my hand reassuringly. "There are signs of a struggle, but other than that no witnesses. We are scheduled to carry out a post mortem today but need you to identify the body, if you feel up to it, of course."

I just nod and the detective looks at me sympathetically. "I'm so sorry, Mrs Carter, this must be extremely difficult for you."

I have no words and just nod as we make our way out of the room and then the building. The detective takes us the short distance to the morgue where Ronnie is waiting and I feel cold and empty inside. I can't shake images of him being brutally murdered while I was happier than I have ever been in my life. It's almost as if this is my punishment for daring to think I could be happy, and I feel disgusted with myself. If only I had listened to him and moved to the North of England, none of this would have happened and he would be alive today. I know I'm being hard on myself, but it's how I feel. Poor Ronnie, he didn't deserve this, and I will do everything in my power to help the police catch the man responsible.

We walk into the sterile room where the bodies are kept and stand beside one of the cold storage units as they unfasten the catch. Julian holds onto me as they slide the body out and as they lift the sheet covering him, I see the lifeless body of the man I loved, battered, bloodied and as cold as ice. He looks strangely serene in death, in direct contrast to how he looked the last time I saw him. Whatever problems he had are now long gone because he is at peace now.

The tears fall fast as I nod and say weakly, "It's him, Ronnie Carter, my husband."

The detective nods and the sheet is replaced and I fall into Julian's arms, sobbing as if my heart is broken.

And when we leave the station, I leave part of that heart behind with Ronnie. How has this happened and why him? I told the detective what I knew. I told him about Caroline and the affair. I told him about Stuart and the threats he made, and I told him about the money and the break in at the house. I told him everything but how I feel because I'm not even sure I know myself. Whatever Ronnie did wasn't bad enough to be murdered over, was it?

34

Julian wants to take me back to the guest house, but I refuse. I need to go home, my real home, and meet with Ronnie's family and sort everything out. He offers to come with me, but I tell him no. It wouldn't be right, and I owe it to Ronnie to deal with this as his wife and not another man's mistress.

So, Julian gives me the space I need and returns home, leaving me to somehow get through this nightmare the right way, as Ronnie deserves.

It's two weeks before the body is released for burial. During that time, the police conduct their enquiries and arrest Stuart and Caroline.

It turns out that she wasn't being straight with me and was as much to blame as her husband. She did have an affair with Ronnie, but Ronnie ended it and told her he wanted to make a go of it with me. That's why he was so desperate to move away where they couldn't find us, and the money in the shoe box was what he saved from gambling. The reason he was murdered was because Caroline had told Stuart he raped her. She was frightened at what he would do to her when he found out she had cheated on him, so made up a terrible story about Ronnie subjecting her to a vicious attack.

Stuart was a violent man with a well-known temper. They had been watching the house, and Caroline was sent in to see if I knew anything. As it turns out, Ronnie did return that night, probably for the money, and they followed him.

He was kept bound and gagged in one of their units and suffered terrible injuries before they stabbed him repeatedly and left his body in the river. Not exactly the crime of the century, but my story helped, along with the DNA leading the police to their door. Caroline confessed everything for a more lenient sentence, which meant the case was wrapped up quickly and cleanly.

However, I am left with the realisation that when Ronnie really needed me; I was too selfish to do as he asked. I put my own needs above my husband's and I will never forgive myself for that.

Julian has tried several times to contact me but I've ignored his calls. I feel too ashamed at what we did while Ronnie was butchered to death and I know I'm being too hard on myself, but I need to mourn in my own way.

Exactly one week after the funeral, I head back to work.

As soon as I walk into Crossline, it feels as if I'm home. The nightmare of the past few weeks hasn't gone away, but I'm in a better place emotionally and feel able to move forward with my life, which I hope includes Julian Landon. I haven't spoken to him and am worried about his reaction when I see him. He will be angry; I know that but I hope he lets me explain myself because if I've come to realise anything, it's that life's too short and I need to grasp my future with both hands.

As I make my way to the executive lift, it's as if I've never been away. Everything looks the same and feels the same. Life goes on, even when it ends for someone important. It almost feels wrong to be walking, talking and eating, but I know I must if I'm to survive.

The lift is full and my fellow workers look at me with curiosity but remain silent. I'm not surprised because I have been away for a long time and they may have heard what happened. Nobody likes to talk about death and loss, illness or anything that raises an emotion in a person they are not equipped to deal with. So, it's with considerable relief that I exit the lift and walk towards Julian's office, steeling myself for the meeting we are about to have.

Will he still want me? The nerves are gripping me tightly as I face the possibility he doesn't. What if he's moved on and found my replacement? I wouldn't blame him because I've been so cold towards him. He's sent flowers, chocolates, notes and messages, but I haven't responded once.

However, as I reach his office door, I take a deep breath and prepare to face the consequences of my actions and knock loudly.

"Come in."

My legs shake as I push the door open and walk inside. Then I blink in disbelief as I see the man watching me approach, smiling slyly as I stare in amazement.

"Good morning, Mrs Carter."

"Mr Slater." My voice is but a whisper as I stare at him in confusion. Then he laughs, a low, hollow sound that tells me everything.

"Take a seat, Mrs Carter, you must be wondering what's going on."

My mouth is dry as I walk towards the chair set before the desk and perch on the edge anxiously.

He leans forward and stares at me with a triumphant look and says relishing every word, "You're fired, Mrs Carter."

I stare at him with a stunned expression and he laughs. "Yes, I have no role for you here, as Louise my own personal assistant is more than willing and able to fill your shoes. In case you are wondering, we have the right to fire you after three months, which is up tomorrow. Sorry that it didn't work out, but these things can't be helped."

My mouth is dry and I can't form words as he pulls a piece of paper from his desk and makes a show of reading it. Then he says in a rough voice, "It appears that you lied on your original application. We checked and you have never worked as the personal assistant of the chief executive of Gascon Industries. You also fabricated paragraphs of your CV that appear to be directly copied from two other much more qualified applicants and we believe you accessed their files through your role as a cleaner here."

I want him to stop, but he is obviously enjoying this way too much as he laughs. "Impressive, Mrs Carter, but extremely foolish. Did you really think an organisation such as this one doesn't check its staff out? I'm surprised that Julian agreed to let you in, but then again, I expect it's because you were screwing him behind his wife's back. Classy, Mrs Carter, very classy, which shows just what lengths you will go to get what you want."

"You're a fine one to talk, Mr Slater."

I feel the fire return as I field his blow with one of my own and he laughs. "Yes, the saying, 'it takes one to know ones,' rings true in our case but I am way cleverer than you because I cover my tracks. In fact, I am so superior to you in every way because you are a nobody, Mrs Carter. You always were and always will be. Now, Harriet will mail your P45 and in the circumstances, I don't believe we can offer you a good recommendation. Just count your blessings that we're not going to prosecute, so get out while I'm still in a good mood."

"What's this, Mr Slater, are you doing Julian's dirty work for him these days?"

Raising his eyes, he looks at me in surprise and laughs softly. "You haven't heard then?"

A cold feeling grips me inside and I stutter, "Heard what?"

"That Julian Landon is currently under investigation for fraud and has been suspended from his role at Crossline while the police investigate. Yes, a lot has happened over the past few weeks, which led to a few changes around here. I am acting CEO and I must say it's been a long time coming. So, if you don't mind, Mrs Carter, I have a lot to do. You will find security waiting to escort you from the premises."

I say no more and leave without looking at his satisfied smirk. Julian is under investigation, for what, I don't understand?

My mind is filled with so much information I can't process it and as I exit the office, I am greeted by Jack who looks a little upset and says kindly, "I'm sorry, Emma. I need your security pass."

Nodding, I hand him the lanyard and walk with him to the lift, my mind working at a million miles an hour.

As we head silently down, he clears his throat and says quietly, "I'm sorry to hear about your husband."

"Thank you." He looks uncomfortable and says kindly, "Would you like me to call you a taxi?"

"No, it's fine, thank you."

We soon reach the ground floor and I walk with him to the revolving doors and he holds out his hand. "Good luck, Emma, I'm sorry it didn't work out."

"Thank you, Jack." I smile, but inside my heart is breaking. How did this happen? I wasn't here for Julian when he needed me, just like Ronnie. I wonder how he is coping?

As I step outside, I take a few deep breaths and try to control my mind. I need to get it together and see if I can be of any help. I can't let Julian down as I did Ronnie, so, grabbing my phone, I call him. However, there is no connection, just the recorded message telling me there is no such number and my heart lurches in fear. He's been cut off.

Suddenly, someone shoves me from behind and I feel myself falling onto the hard pavement below. My phone flies out of my hand and smashes on the ground, and there is a sharp pain in my leg. Looking up, I notice a man towering above me and a familiar voice sneers, "Hello, bitch."

I see a familiar face staring at me with twisted hatred and he sneers, "Look at you cowering on the ground with the filth where you belong. Let me help you up."

I shake my head and make to call for help, but he grabs me in one sharp move and pulls me into a side alley.

He then holds me against the wall by my neck and hisses, "Did you really think I'd let you get away with what you did – bitch?"

I can't even move, but my eyes are wide and terrified as I look into the burning hatred flashing from Declan Cole's hard, unforgiving, eyes.

"You got me fired and I've struggled to find a job as good as that one. But look at you, all dressed up and reaping the rewards of your work in getting me fired. I know it was you and now I'm going to make you pay."

Frantically, I struggle, hoping to free myself just enough to scream. The streets are busy all around us as the workers go about their business, but in this alley, behind a huge bank of waste bins, we may as well be on a desert island.

Declan snarls, "It's about time someone taught you a lesson." He slaps me hard across my face and then I feel him shift my skirt until it is bunched above my waist and he rips off my underwear with a sudden force. My eyes bulge as he holds me firmly against the blackened wall, and I'm terrified as he undoes his trousers. The tears blind me as I wait for the inevitable as he pushes against me. Then I hear, "What the fuck is going on?"

Declan recoils and moves away as a man comes into view. He shouts, "Leave us alone, can't we have a little privacy here?"

The man backs off and says quickly, "I'm going for help."

I'm not surprised he runs because Declan is one huge beast of a man and as he runs off, Declan zips up his trousers and snarls, "I'll be back bitch and next time you won't be so lucky. Look over your shoulder because I'm coming for you."

Then he lands a hard blow to my stomach and the pain is so intense I think I'm about to pass out and slide to the floor in a heap on the ground. I hear him running away and I gasp for air as I realise just what happened. Once again, I hear footsteps and a woman's voice says kindly, "It's ok love, he's gone, you're safe now."

I look up into the kind eyes of a lady who is dressed in the uniform of a nearby restaurant chain.

She looks around and gathers my things and helps me to my feet. "Let me help you, shall I call the police?"

The only thing I want is to get as far away from here as possible, so I shake my head. "No, it's fine."

She hands me my phone and shakes her head. "Bastard. Thank God Mark saw him drag you in here. You should go to the police, dear; the next girl may not be so lucky."

"I will, thank you."

She looks at my phone and shakes her head. "I think you need a new one. Do you want to use mine to call anyone?"

There is only one number I can think of and I'm not sure if he will even answer, but I grab my address book from my bag and nod gratefully. "If it's not too much trouble."

With shaking fingers, I dial Julian's home and wait with bated breath for the phone to ring. Then I hear, "The Landon residence, Nicola speaking."

Almost shaking with nerves, I say falteringly, "Nicola it's Emma, is Julian home?"

There's a short silence and then she says kindly, "Not yet, but he shouldn't be long. Shall I tell him to call you?"

I can't help it and sob, "My phone was smashed, I've been attacked."

"Oh, my goodness, you poor thing, where are you?"

"At the office, I've… I've been fired. Mr Slater, he's told me everything, I'm so sorry."

"Listen, Emma, I'll call you a cab. Come here and wait for Mr Landon."

The relief hits me hard as I sob. "Thank you, oh thank you, Nicola."

I hand the phone back to the kind woman who looks worried. "Why don't you come with me and I'll clean you up. You know, you really should call the police."

Shaking my head, I take a few deep breaths and say with more confidence than I feel. "It's fine, she's sending a car for me. I'll call them from home."

I start to walk away and feel the pain travelling up my leg as I limp out of the alley. My face hurts along with my stomach where he punched me and I feel broken inside. However, I will not fold here outside Crossline and across the street from Barrington's. I will not be a victim and will find a way out of this mess. As the woman follows me out, I say with gratitude. "Thank you…"

"Angela."

"Thank you, Angela, I owe you so much."

She shakes her head and looks unsure about what to do next, and I smile. "I'm fine. I'll just wait for my car, thank you."

She heads off, but I can tell she's uncomfortable leaving me and I sink down onto a nearby bench and wait.

35

The car arrives exactly fifteen minutes later and as it pulls to the kerb, a man jumps out and scans the pavement. Seeing me sitting there exhausted and dishevelled, he heads across and says gently, "Mrs Carter."

Nodding, I look up into the dark brown eyes of a man who looks to be of Arab origin. He smiles kindly and offers me his hand. "Nicola asked me to fetch you. I am Angelo, a friend of hers."

He leads me to the luxury car and settles me into the back before taking the driver's seat and we pull away.

Slumping back in the seat, I let the tears fall as I realise what a lucky escape I just had. It was one thing being fired and escorted from the premises, but nearly being raped by an angry man intent on revenge was on another level entirely.

It hurts everywhere and I am struggling to breathe where he pinned me to the wall by the neck and I'm pretty sure there must be some incredible bruises developing which will show for days, if not weeks.

As the scenery flashes past, I think about Julian and the problems he's now facing. Fraud, but how? If anyone was arrested for fraud, I would have expected it to be Mr Slater. I need to talk to Julian and find out what's going on. Maybe I can help him; I certainly hope he lets me at least.

By the time we turn into the gates of Julian's impressive home, I feel on edge and agitated. What if he throws me out? I will have nothing. No job, no home when I can't make the rent and no prospects without a reference, but most of all, I won't have him, which is the hardest thing of all. Why did I ignore his calls and messages? I was so wrapped up in my own misery, I let the one person down I should have trusted to help me through it all.

The car pulls up outside the huge wooden door and Nicola hurries out.

"Oh, my dear, look what happened to you, come with me."

I feel the ever-present tears building as she helps me from the car and says to the driver, "Check she's left nothing and then you may leave."

She helps me into the impressive home, and I almost cry with relief. I'm safe.

We head for the sumptuous sitting room where she settles me down on the comfortable settee and says firmly, "Right then. I'll fix you a drink for the shock and then run you a bath. You can take the guest house until Mr Landon says otherwise."

"Where is he?" I have to know because I can't see him soon enough and she says kindly. "He won't be long. I've called him and told him what happened."

"But his phone, it was cut off."

"No, his personal one. He'll explain it all when he gets here. Now sit back and relax, I won't be long."

As she hurries from the room, I allow myself to relax for the first time today. He's coming. Thank God. He is just what I need right now and we will deal with this mess together.

Nicola comes back and offers me a glass of something hot that smells like alcohol.

"What is it?"

"Just a tonic, brandy and a little something for the shock. Trust me, it's guaranteed to make you feel much better."

It does smell good, so I take a sip and immediately feel the fiery effects of the liquid as it burns a calming trail to my abused stomach.

I don't need any further invitation and drink it down quicker than I should and lean back and groan. "That's better."

Nicola shakes her head and says angrily, "Look at the state of you. Come with me and we will sort out that bath. Your clothes are still here, so you can change into something more comfortable as soon as you've finished."

It feels good having someone take care of me. Wrapping me up in kindness and taking control.

I follow her to the guest house, feeling much better already and by the time I have the luxurious bath filled with bubbles and shrug on a dressing gown, I feel so tired I almost can't keep my eyes open.

Then she says firmly, "Go and lie down my dear and sleep it off. I'll come and fetch you when Mr Landon returns."

Needing no further invitation, I do as she says and sink into the comfortable king-size bed and drift off to sleep as soon as my head touches the pillow.

36

Something's wrong. I feel it as soon I open my eyes. I can't see anything; there's only darkness. I feel cold and I'm shivering as a draft caresses my body with a chilling breeze. My limbs ache and I'm lying on something cold and hard and the smell - it's overpowering and I can't breathe.

Am I dreaming? I must be because this isn't where I fell asleep, where am I?

Something touches my leg and I open my mouth to scream, but no sound comes out. I'm screaming and screaming, but I must be deaf. I can't hear anything; all I can do is *feel*. My senses are shutting down one by one, and yet I hear the soft breathing of somebody nearby - *someone's here*.

A prickle of fear quickly gains momentum until I feel so afraid, I almost pass out. I feel sick and retch, but nothing happens. I try to move but can't. Am I paralysed or worse – dead?

Where am I? The stench is overpowering me, it smells familiar but I can't place it.

Then the pressure on my leg increases and I hear a soft, "She's coming round."

I try to put a face to the voice, but it all seems so distant. Then I hear a man's voice, louder, more urgent. "We don't have long."

What's happening, where am I?

Then I feel a liquid running down my leg that burns and I scream and this time my voice works, although it's weaker than normal. A sharp voice hisses, "Shut up, we are just cleaning you up to prepare you for transit."

Transit, what the hell is happening, who are these people?

I want to be sick; the smell is too intense and I retch. Then I feel a calm hand on my forehead and the man says, "She's burning up, how much did you give her?"

"The usual dose; she'll be fine."

I feel her hands all over me now. Scrubbing, kneading, burning and torturing. They move to my stomach and I wince as the pain grips me and she says angrily, "She's damaged; they may reject her."

"No, they won't care. She'll look a lot worse by the time they've finished with her."

I can't move and I can't talk. What the hell is happening?

I start to shiver, I am so cold, so sick and in so much pain it consumes my entire body. It's too intense and I can't breathe. What is that smell?

Then I hear, "It's done, you can bring the truck around."

I hear movement, loud noises and the scraping of a heavy object across a concrete floor. The cold is intense and the pain hurts from the inside out.

Then I hear a whisper, a soft sound in my ear as she says, "It's time to go."

Go where, what is she talking about?

Somebody is lifting me, but still I can't move. Then another grabs my head and pulls it back by my hair. I cry out in pain and then the light hits me, blinding me as something is torn from my eyes. *I can see again.*

As my eyes focus and their faces swim into view, I stare at them in shock. "You!"

Nicola smiles. "Yes dear, only me, nothing to worry about."

But who? I try to twist my head to see my captor and she smiles. "It's just Angelo, he's here to deliver you."

"Deliver me, what are you talking about?"

My skin burns and I say in disbelief, "What's happening?"

"Nothing personal dear, just business. You see, it was lucky you called, really. For me, anyway. I've had an order waiting for a while now and nobody to send. Then you came along with your tale of woe and nobody to turn to and I saw my chance."

"What chance? Please tell me what's happening."

She laughs and yet it sounds brutal and cold. "As I said, just business. You see, for a while now, I've had a little side business that's quite lucrative. I provide girls with no baggage to friends of Angelo's for certain parties they arrange. They use the goods I send them and pay me well for my trouble. Very well as it happens and then I get paid all over again by the next customer."

I stare into the eyes of a madwoman as she laughs again. "Then I sell what's left of you for spare parts, shall we say. People that need what you no longer have use for."

She runs her hands over my chest and says, "Heart, kidneys, eyes, oh the list is endless and I make quite a *killing* on the black market."

The panic takes over and I open my mouth to scream and as I do, she places her hand over my mouth and sinks a needle into my arm. "Sleep well my dear, like I said, it's nothing personal, just business."

37

I hear voices and this time I feel warm. There is something soft beneath me and there is no pain. I move slightly and someone says, "She's coming round."

Then the fear grips me. Where am? What are they going to do to me?

I jerk and I hear louder voices and one that I recognise. "For fuck's sake do something."

It brings a smile to my lips and then I hear no more.

The next time I wake, I feel someone stroking my head and it feels nice. My eyelids flicker and he says, "Emma, it's me, Julian. Blink if you can hear me."

I open my eyes and his face swims into view. He looks concerned, worried, angry. All of those things that make him mine.

He smiles and I see tears in his eyes as he whispers, "I almost lost you."

He calls out, "Nurse, she's back."

I hear movement and then another face joins his and smiles. "Hi, Emma, I'm Marion Davey and you're safe in hospital. Try not to speak and we'll just run some tests."

For a while I am happy to let them do their job and all that concerns me doesn't leave my side throughout.

Julian holds my hand and tells me how much he loves me; how scared he's been and that I'm not to worry about anything ever because he's not leaving me again.

Much later, I finally get to hear what happened.

I am sitting up in my hospital bed in a private room and have been told I'm to be discharged shortly. I've just finished a meal of soup and crusty bread and have never tasted anything so good in my life.

Julian is sitting beside me looking as if he's been through hell and back and I say, "Well, what happened?"

The pain fills his eyes and he says, "It was a good thing you were out of the way because the shit really hit the fan when Cressida was served her divorce papers. The day we left her in the kitchen, I told her I knew about her deal with Slater and that I found her retirement fund and the police would be informed. Unless she agreed to divorce me, I would prosecute and she would lose everything. She denied it, of course, and told me she was just sleeping with him but when I told her there were witnesses, she broke down – finally. She told me he agreed to help her frame and discredit me. They would make it so I was the one in the firing line for insider dealing and manipulating the stock market. They had been very careful to cover the tracks that could easily be redirected to my door, especially as I had been the one to benefit from their scam. Then

I told her about the money in the retirement fund, and I had handed it over to my solicitor. She denied all knowledge of it and as it turns out she was right."

"Nicola?"

He nods grimly. "Yes, she had access to our computer and discovered Cressida's password. She used her details to open an account and transfer the funds from her 'business' therefore incriminating Cressida if she was ever discovered."

"She used Amelia's name because she knew Cressida wouldn't notice."

"Yes, Cressida isn't one for sentiment and wouldn't have been remotely interested in anything professing to be made up of her daughters' memories, so Nicola used it to disguise the transactions. Cressida hates computers, anyway, and always delegated her admin to Nicola, so she was pretty safe from being found out. You can say what you want about my now ex-wife, but she will always admit the truth when backed into a corner. So, I handed the lot over to the police who have pulled it apart with a fine-tooth comb."

"But Slater, he told me you'd been suspended for the same crime you are saying he carried out."

"It was a set up. The police agreed I would act as a decoy and allow Slater to think his plan had worked. We bugged the office and his private phone, and it wasn't long before he gave himself away. The day he fired you was the day they moved in. He's now on remand in prison awaiting trial and we thought that was an end to it."

I look down and almost can't say the words because what could have happened is so frightening. "How did you find me?"

"The police again. They looked into Cressida's retirement fund and traced the transactions. They all pointed to a bank in Switzerland that belonged to a man called Omar Naser Abbas. It turns out he was Nicola's previous employer and she had worked for him for ten years in Qatar. The police put a tail on her and then went back over their records and noticed the transactions tied in with a spate of missing girls from the area. They investigated the private airfields for any flights that left to the middle east around those dates and narrowed it down to the local one. It all added up and they sent in surveillance. The day you were supposed to be..."

He breaks off looking upset and I say gently, "Sold." He nods. "They intercepted the pair at the airfield and arrested them. They are also on remand and if I have my way, will never see the outside of a prison again."

"Those poor girls." I look down and the tears spill for the girls that were reported missing. Thinking of their fate, which could have so easily been mine, makes my blood freeze. I almost can't speak, such is the horror running through my mind and Julian says softly, "You can't think about it. It never happened, to you, anyway and I will pay for as much counselling as you need to make sure you get through this."

He comes and sits beside me and takes me in his arms. "I want to care for you, Emma. I want to be by your side for the rest of our lives and will spend mine making this right. What happened to you is the stuff of nightmares, and I can't imagine how you must be feeling. Please, let me love you, darling, don't turn away from me."

Reaching up, I cup his face in my hand and say softly, "I'm going nowhere - deal with it."

Grinning wickedly, he kisses me gently and with so much love, my heart flutters. Suddenly, I know what life is all about. It's not the money, the power, the nice home and material possessions. It's this. The love of one person for another and a life shared. Caring for each other through thick and thin and making each other a better person along the way. Now I can move out of the shadows and dance in the light. Today is the beginning of the rest of my life and I am not going to waste a second of it.

Epilogue

Two years later.

"Hi, Emma."

"Hi, Louise, is he in?"

She nods and rolls her eyes and I smile. "That bad, huh?"

"A little grouchy today."

We giggle and I shake my head. "I'm sorry, what's his problem today?"

"One of the new traders messed up a transaction and lost the client a shed load of money. Mr Landon's been trying to fight the fire all morning and it's a brave person that ventures in there."

"Then it's a good job I'm fearless."

She laughs. "Anybody but you. I don't know how you do it."

I wink and she giggles. Louise took my position at my recommendation and I took over caring for Amelia and Imogen. I am much happier taking care of my ready-made family, and even though it's not for everyone, I've discovered that I'm at my happiest taking care of them. Cressida lives in Florida with her new fiancé and the girls visit her on holidays and she flies in for the occasional weekend. We don't have much to do with her, but we've found our way and it's civil at least.

Julian and I married after just six months, with the girls as bridesmaids and two strangers acting as witnesses in Antigua. Our little family is all we want and we treasure it above everything else.

Knocking loudly, I hear a terse, "For fuck's sake, I told you I didn't want to be disturbed."

Pushing my way in, I stand regarding my husband who looks up and rolls his eyes. "Thank fuck it's you. These bastards are seriously pissing me off."

"Mind your language. You're getting worse. Anything I can help you with?"

He nods. "You can try."

Grabbing the spare chair in the corner that I know so well; I drag it to his side and study the screen. He points out where the transaction went wrong and we are soon working out ways to limit the damage for the client.

Julian has taken great pains to educate me on the way things work, and I was a willing student. We love nothing more than poring over stocks and shares and working out ways to increase our customer's profits by way of anticipating the markets. Finally, my detective skills count for something good rather than bad and we have become quite good at it. I even have my own trading account that I work on from what is now *our* office at home and have built up my own considerable fortune.

In the aftermath of what happened, I went to live with Julian and we worked it through. Somehow, we got through the dark times and now the future is bright. We still live in the sprawling mansion but are careful with our money. The guest house where Nicola 'prepared' me for sale has been knocked down and a tennis court now stands proudly where it once was. The terrible smell that overpowered me that day was industrial bleach, which I still, to this day, have no idea why they used it. Julian believes it was to strip away any DNA that would lead them back to Nicola, which is probably the most likely explanation.

By the time we finish studying the account, it's getting dark and I stretch out. "It's a good job the girls are at a sleepover, that was good timing."

He spins my chair to face his and says huskily, "I have plans for you this evening and we are wasting time."

"You do? May I ask what?"

He grins and leans forward, saying huskily, "I think I want to make baby number three."

"You always want to make baby number three."

"And you always refuse me, why?"

"Because of the girls. I don't want them to feel upset if we have a baby of our own."

He kisses me softly and smiles. "They have pleaded for months for a baby to play with, that's a rubbish excuse. Why are you really stalling?"

To be honest, I can't answer him because I don't even know myself. I suppose because my life is so perfect now, I don't want anything to change. However, as I look into those eyes that always drew me in, I see how lucky I am. Julian loves me unconditionally and why wouldn't I want a miniature version of him running around?

I laugh and he looks surprised. "What's so funny?"

"I just imagined a miniature you running around, god forbid. Maybe this is God's way of telling me to back off, the world isn't ready for another Julian Landon terrorising the workers."

He grins and pulls me closer and whispers, "What if it's a miniature version of Emma Landon. The world could do with another one of those."

"Then what are we waiting for, let's go and make a baby."

As we kiss, it suddenly seems like the most natural thing in the world. Yes, it's time to add to our family and bring a new life into the world. After all, isn't that the only dream that matters?

The End

Thank you for reading The Grey Woman. If you have enjoyed the story, I would be so grateful if you could post a review on Amazon. It really helps other readers when deciding what to read and means everything to the Author who wrote it.

Connect with me on Facebook

Check out my website sjcrabb.com

READ ON FOR MORE BOOKS BY M J HARDY

HAVE YOU READ?

Learn More

The Girl on Gander Green Lane

The Husband Thief

Living the Dream

The Woman who Destroyed Christmas

Thank you

I feel very fortunate that my stories continue to delight my readers. The Girl on Gander Green Lane reached the number 1 spot in Australia in the entire Kindle Store. The Husband Thief and The Woman who Destroyed Christmas reached the top 100 in Canada, the UK and Australia.

I couldn't do it without your support and I thank each one of you who has supported me.
For those of you who don't know, I also write under another name. S J Crabb.
You will find my books at sjcrabb.com where they all live side by side.
As an Independent Author I take huge pride in my business and if anything, it shows what one individual can achieve if they work hard enough.
I will continue to write stories that I hope you will enjoy, so make sure to follow me on Amazon, or sign up to my Newsletter, or like my Facebook page, so you are informed of any new releases.

With lots of love and thanks.

Sharon xx (M J Hardy)

Printed by Amazon Italia Logistica S.r.l.
Torrazza Piemonte (TO), Italy